THE WORLD 100 YEARS AGO

EGYPT

THE WORLD 100 YEARS AGO

BERLIN

EGYPT

THE CITIES OF JAPAN

LONDON

MOSCOW

PARIS

PEKING

SOUTHERN ITALY

THE WORLD 100 YEARS AGO

BURTON HOLMES
EGYPT

FRED L. ISRAEL
General Editor

ARTHUR M. SCHLESINGER, JR.
Senior Consulting Editor

CHELSEA HOUSE PUBLISHERS
Philadelphia

CHELSEA HOUSE PUBLISHERS
EDITOR-IN-CHIEF Stephen Reginald
MANAGING EDITOR James D. Gallagher
PRODUCTION MANAGER Pamela Loos
ART DIRECTOR Sara Davis
PICTURE EDITOR Judy Hasday
SENIOR PRODUCTION EDITOR Lisa Chippendale
ASSOCIATE ART DIRECTOR Takeshi Takahashi
COVER DESIGN Dave Loose Design

Copyright © 1998 by Chelsea House Publishers, a division of Main Line Book Co. All rights reserved. Printed and bound in the United States of America.

First Printing

1 3 5 7 9 8 6 4 2

Library of Congress Cataloging-in-Publication Data

Holmes, Burton, b. 1870.
Egypt/ by Burton Holmes; Fred L. Israel, general editor; Arthur M. Schlesinger, jr., senior consulting editor.
  p. cm. —(World 100 years ago)
Includes index.

ISBN 0-7910-4670-2 (hc) ISBN 0-7910-4671-0 (pb).

1. Egypt—Description and travel. 2. Holmes, Burton, b. 1870—Journeys—Egypt. I. Israel, Fred L.
II. Schlesinger, Arthur Meier, 1917- . III. Title.
IV. Series: Holmes, Burton, b. 1870. World 100 years ago today.
DT56.2.H65   1997
916.204'4—dc21   97-36296
                                                        CIP

Contents

The Great Globe Trotter *Irving Wallace*	6
Burton Holmes *Arthur M. Schlesinger, jr.*	24
The World 100 Years Ago *Dr. Fred Israel*	26
Egypt	35
Further Reading	170
Contributors	171
Index	172

THE GREAT GLOBE TROTTER

By Irving Wallace

One day in the year 1890, Miss Nellie Bly, of the *New York World,* came roaring into Brooklyn on a special train from San Francisco. In a successful effort to beat Phileas Fogg's fictional 80 days around the world, Miss Bly, traveling with two handbags and flannel underwear, had circled the globe in 72 days, 6 hours, and 11 minutes. Immortality awaited her.

Elsewhere that same year, another less-publicized globe-girdler made his start toward immortality. He was Mr. Burton Holmes, making his public debut with slides and anecdotes ("Through Europe With a Kodak") before the Chicago Camera Club. Mr. Holmes, while less spectacular than his feminine rival, was destined, for that very reason, soon to dethrone her as America's number-one traveler.

Today, Miss Bly and Mr. Holmes have one thing in common: In the mass mind they are legendary vagabonds relegated to the dim and dusty past of the Iron Horse and the paddle-wheel steamer. But if Miss Bly, who shuffled off this mortal coil in 1922, is now only a part of our folklore, there are millions to testify that

Mr. Burton Holmes, aged seventy-six, is still very much with us.

Remembering that Mr. Holmes was an active contemporary of Miss Bly's, that he was making a livelihood at traveling when William McKinley, John L. Sullivan, and Admiral Dewey ruled the United States, when Tony Pastor, Lily Langtry, and Lillian Russell ruled the amusement world, it is at once amazing and reassuring to pick up the daily newspapers of 1946 and find, sandwiched between advertisements of rash young men lecturing on "Inside Stalin" and "I Was Hitler's Dentist," calm announcements that tomorrow evening Mr. Burton Holmes has something more to say about "Beautiful Bali."

Burton Holmes, a brisk, immaculate, chunky man with gray Vandyke beard, erect bearing, precise speech ("folks are always mistaking me for Monty Woolley," he says, not unhappily), is one of the seven wonders of the entertainment world. As Everyman's tourist, Burton Holmes has crossed the Atlantic Ocean thirty times, the Pacific Ocean twenty times, and has gone completely around the world six times. He has spent fifty-five summers abroad, and recorded a half million feet of film of those summers. He was the first person to take motion picture cameras into Russia and Japan. He witnessed the regular decennial performance of the Passion Play at Oberammergau in 1890, and attended the first modern Olympics at Athens in 1896. He rode on the first Trans-Siberian train across Russia, and photographed the world's first airplane meet at Rheims.

As the fruit of these travels, Burton Holmes has delivered approximately 8,000 illustrated lectures that have grossed, according to an estimate by *Variety,* five million dollars in fifty-three winters. Because he does not like to be called a lecturer—"I'm a performer," he insists, "and I have performed on more legitimate stages than platforms"—he invented the word "travelogue" in London to describe his activity.

His travelogues, regarded as a fifth season of the year in most communities, have won him such popularity that he holds the record for playing in the longest one-man run in American show business. In the five and a half decades past, Burton Holmes has successively met the hectic competition of big-time vaudeville, stage, silent pictures, radio, and talking pictures, and he has survived them all.

At an age when most men have retired to slippered ease or are hounded by high blood pressure, Burton Holmes is more active and more popular than ever before. In the season just finished, which he started in San Francisco during September, 1945, and wound up in New York during April, 1946, Holmes appeared in 187 shows, a record number. He averaged six travelogues a week, spoke for two hours at each, and did 30 percent more box-office business than five years ago. Not once was a scheduled lecture postponed or canceled. In fact, he has missed only two in his life. In 1935, flying over the Dust Bowl, he suffered laryngitis and was forced to bypass two college dates. He has never canceled an appearance before a paid city audience. Seven years ago, when one of his elderly limbs was fractured in an automobile crack-up in Finland, there was a feeling that Burton Holmes might not make the rounds. When news of the accident was released, it was as if word had gone out that Santa Claus was about to cancel his winter schedule. But when the 1939 season dawned, Burton Holmes rolled on the stage in a wheelchair, and from his seat of pain (and for 129 consecutive appearances thereafter), he delivered his travel chat while 16-mm film shimmered on the screen beside him.

Today, there is little likelihood that anything, except utter extinction, could keep Holmes from his waiting audiences. Even now, between seasons, Holmes is in training for his next series—150 illustrated lectures before groups in seventeen states.

Before World War II, accompanied by Margaret Oliver, his wife of thirty-two years, Holmes would spend his breathing spells on summery excursions through the Far East or Europe. While aides captured scenery on celluloid, Holmes wrote accompanying lecture material in his notebooks. Months later, he would communicate his findings to his cult, at a maximum price of $1.50 per seat. With the outbreak of war, Holmes changed his pattern. He curtailed travel outside the Americas. This year, except for one journey to Las Vegas, Nevada, where he personally photographed cowboy cutups and shapely starlets at the annual Helldorado festival, Holmes has been allowing his assistants to do all his traveling for him.

Recently, one crew, under cameraman Thayer Soule, who helped shoot the Battle of Tarawa for the Marines, brought Holmes a harvest of new film from Mexico. Another crew, after four months in Brazil last year, and two in its capital this year, returned to Holmes with magnificent movies. Meantime, other crews, under assignment from Holmes, are finishing films on Death Valley, the West Indies, and the Mississippi River.

In a cottage behind his sprawling Hollywood hilltop home, Holmes is busy, day and night, sorting the incoming negative, cutting and editing it, and rewriting lectures that will accompany the footage this winter. He is too busy to plan his next trip. Moreover, he doesn't feel that he should revisit Europe yet. "I wouldn't mind seeing it," he says, "but I don't think my public would be interested. My people want a good time, they want escape, they want sweetness and light, beauty and charm. There is too much rubble and misery over there now, and I'll let those picture magazines and Fox Movietone newsreels show all that. I'll wait until it's tourist time again."

When he travels, he thinks he will visit three of the four accessible places on earth that he has not yet seen. One is Tahiti, which he barely missed a dozen times, and the other two are Iran and Iraq. The remaining country that he has not seen, and has no wish to see, is primitive Afghanistan. Of all cities on earth, he would most like to revisit Kyoto, once capital of Japan. He still recalls that the first movies ever made inside Japan were ones he made in Kyoto, in 1899. The other cities he desires to revisit are

Venice and Rome. The only island for which he has any longing is Bali—"the one quaint spot on earth where you can really get away from it all."

In preparing future subjects, Holmes carefully studies the success of his past performances. Last season, his two most popular lectures in the East were "California" and "Adventures in Mexico." The former grossed $5,100 in two Chicago shows; the latter jammed the St. Louis Civic Auditorium with thirty-five hundred potential señores and señoritas. Holmes will use these subjects again, with revisions, next season, and add some brand-new Latin American and United States topics. He will sidestep anything relating to war. He feels, for example, that anything dealing with the once exotic Pacific islands might have a questionable reception—"people will still remember those white crosses they saw in newsreels of Guadalcanal and Iwo Jima."

Every season presents its own obstacles, and the next will challenge Holmes with a new audience of travel-sated and disillusioned ex-GI's. Many of these men, and their families, now know that a South Sea island paradise means mosquitoes and malaria and not Melville's Fayaway and Loti's Rarahu. They know Europe means mud and ruins and not romance. Nevertheless, Holmes is confident that he will win these people over.

"The veterans of World War II will come to my travelogues just as their fathers did. After the First World War, I gave illustrated lectures on the sights of France, and the ex-doughboys enjoyed them immensely. But I suppose there's no use comparing that war to this. The First World War was a minor dispute between gentlemen. In this one, the atrocities and miseries will be difficult to forget. I know I can't give my Beautiful Italy lecture next season to men who know Italy only as a pigsty, but you see, in my heart Italy is forever beautiful, and I see things in Italy they can't see, poor fellows. How could they? . . . Still, memory is frail, and one day these boys will forget and come to my lectures not to hoot but to relive the better moments and enjoy themselves."

While Burton Holmes prepares his forthcoming shows, his business manager, a slightly built dynamo named Walter Everest, works on next season's bookings. Everest contacts organizations interested in sponsoring a lecture series, arranges dates and prices, and often leases auditoriums on his own. Everest concentrates on cities where Holmes is known to be popular, Standing Room Only cities like New York, Boston, Philadelphia, Chicago, Los Angeles. On the other hand, he is cautious about the cities where Holmes has been unpopular in the past—Toledo, Cleveland, Indianapolis, Cincinnati. The one city Holmes now avoids entirely is Pomona, California, where, at a scheduled Saturday matinee, he found himself facing an almost empty house. The phenomenon of a good city or a poor city is inexplicable. In rare cases, there may be a reason for failure, and then Holmes will attempt to resolve it. When San Francisco was stone-deaf to Holmes, investigation showed that he had been competing with the annual opera season. Last year, he rented a theater the week before the opera began. He appeared eight times and made a handsome profit.

Once Holmes takes to the road for his regular season, he is a perpetual-motion machine. Leaving his wife behind, he barnstorms with his manager, Everest, and a projectionist, whirling to Western dates in his Cadillac, making long hops by plane, following the heavier Eastern circuit by train. Holmes likes to amaze younger men with his activities during a typical week. If he speaks in Detroit on a Tuesday night, he will lecture in Chicago on Wednesday evening, in Milwaukee on Thursday, be back in Chicago for Friday evening and a Saturday matinee session, then go on to Kansas City on Sunday, St. Louis on Monday, and play a return engagement in Detroit on Tuesday.

This relentless merry-go-round (with Saturday nights off to attend a newsreel "and see what's happening in the world") invigorates Holmes, but grinds his colleagues to a frazzle. One morning last season, after weeks of trains and travel, Walter

Everest was awakened by a porter at six. He rose groggily, sat swaying on the edge of his berth trying to put on his shoes. He had the look of a man who had pushed through the Matto Grosso on foot. He glanced up sleepily, and there, across the aisle, was Holmes, fully dressed, looking natty and refreshed. Holmes smiled sympathetically. "I know, Walter," he said, "this life is tiring. One day both of us ought to climb on some train and get away from it all."

In his years on the road, Holmes has come to know his audience thoroughly. He is firm in the belief that it is composed mostly of traveled persons who wish to savor the glamorous sights of the world again. Through Burton, they relive their own tours. Of the others, some regard a Holmes performance as a preview. They expect to travel; they want to know the choice sights for their future three-month jaunt to Ecuador. Some few, who consider themselves travel authorities, come to a Holmes lecture to point out gleefully the good things that he missed. "It makes them happy," Holmes says cheerfully. Tomorrow's audience, for the most, will be the same as the one that heard the Master exactly a year before. Generations of audiences inherit Holmes, one from the other.

An average Holmes lecture combines the atmosphere of a revival meeting and a family get-together at which home movies are shown. A typical Holmes travelogue begins in a brightly lit auditorium, at precisely three minutes after eight-thirty. The three minutes is to allow for latecomers. Holmes, attired in formal evening clothes, strides from the wings to center stage. People applaud; some cheer. Everyone seems to know him and to know exactly what to expect. Holmes smiles broadly. He is compact, proper, handsome. His goatee dominates the scene. He has worn it every season, with the exception of one in 1895 (when, beardless, he somewhat resembled Paget's Sherlock Holmes). Now, he speaks crisply. He announces that this is the third lecture of his fifty-fourth season. He announces his subject—"Adventures in Mexico."

He walks to one side of the stage, where a microphone is standing. The lights are dimmed. The auditorium becomes dark. Beyond the fifth row, Holmes cannot be seen. The all-color 16-mm film is projected on the screen. The film opens, minus title and credits, with a shot through the windshield of an automobile speeding down the Pan-American Highway to Monterrey. Holmes himself is the sound track. His speech, with just the hint of a theatrical accent, is intimate, as if he were talking in a living room. He punctuates descriptive passages with little formal jokes. When flowers and orange trees of Mexico are on the screen, he says, "We have movies and talkies, but now we should have smellies and tasties"—and he chuckles.

The film that he verbally captions is a dazzling, uncritical montage of Things Mexican. There is a señora selling tortillas, and close-ups of how tortillas are made. There is a bullfight, but not the kill. There is snow-capped Popocatepetl, now for sale at the bargain price of fifteen million dollars. There are the pyramids outside Mexico City, older than those of Egypt, built by the ancient Toltecs who went to war with wooden swords so that they would not kill their enemies.

Holmes's movies and lectures last two hours, with one intermission. The emphasis is on description, information, and oddity. Two potential ingredients are studiously omitted. One is adventure, the other politics. Holmes is never spectacular. "I want nothing dangerous. I don't care to emulate the explorers, to risk my neck, to be the only one or the first one there. Let others tackle the Himalayas, the Amazon, the North Pole, let them break the trails for me. I'm just a Cook's tourist, a little ahead of the crowd, but not too far ahead." Some years ago, Holmes did think that he was an explorer, and became very excited about it, he now admits sheepishly. This occurred in a trackless sector of Northern Rhodesia. Holmes felt that he had discovered a site never before seen by an outsider. Grandly, he planted the flag of the Explorers

Club, carefully he set up his camera, and then, as he prepared to shoot, his glance fell upon an object several feet away—an empty Kodak carton. Quietly, he repacked and stole away—and has stayed firmly on the beaten paths ever since.

As to politics, it never taints his lectures. He insists neither he nor his audiences are interested. "When you discuss politics," he says, "you are sure to offend." Even after his third trip to Russia, he refused to discuss politics. "I am a traveler," he explained at that time, "and not a student of political and economic questions. To me, Communism is merely one of the sights I went to see."

However, friends know that Holmes has his pet panacea for the ills of the world. He is violent about the gold standard, insisting that it alone can make all the world prosperous. Occasionally, when the mood is on him, and against his better judgment, he will inject propaganda in favor of the gold standard into an otherwise timid travelogue.

When he is feeling mellow, Holmes will confess that once in the past he permitted politics to intrude upon his sterile chitchat. It was two decades ago, when he jousted with Prohibition. While not a dedicated drinking man, Holmes has been on a friendly basis with firewater since the age of sixteen. In the ensuing years, he has regularly, every dusk before dinner, mixed himself one or two highballs. Only once did he try more than two, and the results were disastrous. "Any man who drinks three will drink three hundred," he now says righteously. Holmes felt that Prohibition was an insult to civilized living. As a consequence of this belief, his audiences during the days of the Eighteenth Amendment were often startled to hear Holmes extol the virtues of open drinking, in the middle of a placid discourse on Oberammergau or Lapland. "Sometimes an indignant female would return her tickets to the rest of my series," he says, "but there were others, more intelligent, to take her place."

This independent attitude in Holmes was solely the product of his personal success. Born in January, 1870, of a financially secure, completely cosmopolitan Chicago family, he was able to be independent from his earliest days. His father, an employee in the Third National Bank, distinguished himself largely by lending George Pullman enough cash to transform his old day coaches into the first Pullman Palace Sleeping Cars, and by refusing a half interest in the business in exchange for his help. Even to this day, it makes Burton Holmes dizzy to think of the money he might have saved in charges for Pullman berths.

Holmes's interest in show business began at the age of nine when his grandmother, Ann W. Burton, took him to hear John L. Stoddard lecture on the Passion Play at Oberammergau. Young Holmes was never the same again. After brief visits to faraway Florida and California, he quit school and accompanied his grandmother on his first trip abroad. He was sixteen and wide-eyed. His grandmother, who had traveled with her wine-salesman husband to France and Egypt and down the Volga in the sixties, was the perfect guide. But this journey through Europe was eclipsed, four years later, by a more important pilgrimage with his grandmother to Germany. The first day at his hotel in Munich, Holmes saw John L. Stoddard pass through the lobby reading a Baedeker. He was petrified. It was as if he had seen his Maker. Even now, over a half century later, when Holmes speaks about Stoddard, his voice carries a tinge of awe. For eighteen years of the later nineteenth century, Stoddard, with black-and-white slides and magnificent oratory, dominated the travel-lecture field. To audiences, young and old, he was the most romantic figure in America. Later, at Oberammergau, Holmes sat next to Stoddard through the fifteen acts of the Passion Play and they became friends.

When Holmes returned to the States, some months after Nellie Bly had made her own triumphal return to Brooklyn, he showed rare Kodak negatives of his travels to fellow members of the Chicago Camera Club. The members were impressed, and one suggested that these be mounted as slides and shown to the general public. "To take the edge off the silence, to keep the show moving," says Holmes, "I wrote an account of my journey and read it, as the stereopticon man changed slides." The show, which grossed the club $350, was Holmes's initial travelogue. However, he dates the beginning of his professional career from three years later, when he appeared under his own auspices with hand-colored slides.

After the Camera Club debut, Holmes did not go immediately into the travelogue field. He was not yet ready to appreciate its possibilities. Instead, he attempted to sell real estate, and failed. Then he worked for eight dollars a week as a photo supply clerk. In 1902, aching with wanderlust, he bullied his family into staking him to a five-month tour of Japan. On the boat he was thrilled to find John L. Stoddard, also bound for Japan. They became closer friends, even though they saw Nippon through different eyes. "The older man found Japan queer, quaint, comfortless, and almost repellent," Stoddard's son wrote years later. "To the younger man it was a fairyland." Stoddard invited Holmes to continue on around the world with him, but Holmes loved Japan and decided to remain.

When Holmes returned to Chicago, the World's Columbian Exposition of 1893 was in full swing. He spent months at the Jackson Park grounds, under Edison's new electric lights, listening to Lillian Russell sing, Susan B. Anthony speak, and watching Sandow perform feats of strength. With rising excitement, he observed Jim Brady eating, Anthony Comstock snorting at Little Egypt's hootchy-kootchy, and Alexander Dowie announcing himself as the Prophet Elijah III.

In the midst of this excitement came the depression of that year. Holmes's father suffered. "He hit the wheat pit at the wrong time, and I had to go out on my own," says Holmes. "The photo supply house offered me fifteen dollars a week to return. But I didn't want to work. The trip to Japan, the Oriental exhibits of the Exposition, were still on my mind. I thought of

Stoddard. I thought of the slides I'd had hand-colored in Tokyo. That was it, and it wasn't work. So I hired a hall and became a travel lecturer."

Copying society addresses from his mother's visiting list, and additional addresses from *The Blue Book,* Holmes mailed two thousand invitations in the form of Japanese poem-cards. Recipients were invited to two illustrated lectures, at $1.50 each, on "Japan—the Country and the Cities." Both performances were sellouts. Holmes grossed $700.

For four years Holmes continued his fight to win a steady following, but with only erratic success. Then, in 1897, when he stood at the brink of defeat, two events occurred to change his life. First, John L. Stoddard retired from the travel-lecture field and threw the platforms of the nation open to a successor. Second, Holmes supplemented colored slides with a new method of illustrating his talks. As his circular announced, "There will be presented for the first time in connection with a course of travel lectures a series of pictures to which a modern miracle has added the illusion of life itself—the reproduction of recorded motion."

Armed with his jumpy movies—scenes of the Omaha fire department, a police parade in Chicago, Italians eating spaghetti, each reel running twenty-five seconds, with a four-minute wait between reels—Burton Holmes invaded the Stoddard strongholds in the East. Stoddard came to hear him and observe the newfangled movies. Like Marshal Foch who regarded the airplane as "an impractical toy," Stoddard saw no future in the motion picture. Nevertheless, he gave young Holmes a hand by insisting that Augustin Daly lease his Manhattan theater to the newcomer. This done, Stoddard retired to the Austrian Tyrol, and Holmes went on to absorb Stoddard's audiences in Boston and Philadelphia and to win new followers of his own throughout the nation.

His success assured, Holmes began to gather material with a vigor that was to make him one of history's most indefatigable travelers. In 1900, at the Paris Exposition, sitting in a restaurant built like a Russian train, drinking vodka while a colored panorama of Siberia rolled past his window, he succumbed to this unique advertising of the new Trans-Siberian railway and bought a ticket. The trip in 1901 was a nightmare. After ten days on the Trans-Siberian train, which banged along at eleven miles an hour, Holmes was dumped into a construction train for five days, and then spent twenty-seven days on steamers going down the Amur River. It took him forty-two and a half days to travel from Moscow to Vladivostok.

But during that tour, he had one great moment. He saw Count Leo Tolstoi at Yasnaya Polyana, the author's country estate near Tula. At a dinner in Moscow, Holmes met Albert J. Beveridge, the handsome senator from Indiana. Beveridge had a letter of introduction to Tolstoi and invited Holmes and his enormous 60-mm movie camera to come along. Arriving in a four-horse landau, the Americans were surprised to find Tolstoi's house dilapidated. Then, they were kept waiting two hours. At last, the seventy-three-year-old, white-bearded Tolstoi, nine years away from his lonely death in a railway depot, appeared. He was attired in a mujik costume. He invited his visitors to breakfast, then conversed in fluent English. "He had only a slight accent, and he spoke with the cadence of Sir Henry Irving," Holmes recalls.

Of the entire morning's conversation, Holmes remembers clearly only one remark. That was when Tolstoi harangued, "There should be no law. No man should have the right to judge or condemn another. Absolute freedom of the individual is the only thing that can redeem the world. Christ was a great teacher, nothing more!" As Tolstoi continued to speak, Holmes quietly set up his movie camera. Tolstoi had never seen one before. He posed stiffly, as for a daguerreotype. When he thought that it was over, and resumed his talking, Holmes began actual shooting. This priceless film never reached the screen. Senator Beveridge was then a presidential possibility. His managers feared that this film of Beveridge with a Russian radical might be used by his opponents. The film was taken from Holmes and destroyed. Later, when he was not even nominated for the presidency, Beveridge wrote an apology to Holmes, "for this destruction of so valuable a living record of the grand old Russian."

In 1934, at a cost of ten dollars a day, Holmes spent twenty-one days in modern Soviet Russia. He loved the ballet, the omelets, the Russian rule against tipping, and the lack of holdups. He went twice to see the embalmed Lenin, fascinated by the sight of "his head resting on a red pillow like that of a tired man asleep."

Although Holmes's name had already appeared on eighteen travel volumes, this last Russian trip inspired him to write his first and only original book. The earlier eighteen volumes, all heavily illustrated, were offered as a set, of which over forty thousand were sold. However, they were not "written," but were actually a collection of lectures delivered orally by Holmes. The one book that he wrote as a book, *The Traveler's Russia,* published in 1934 by G.P. Putnam's Sons, was a failure. Holmes has bought the remainders and passes them out to guests with a variety of inscriptions. In a serious mood he will inscribe, "To travel is to possess the world." In a frivolous mood, he will write "With love from Tovarich Burtonovich Holmeski."

In the five decades past, Holmes has kept himself occupied with a wide variety of pleasures, such as attending Queen Victoria's Golden Jubilee in London, chatting with Admiral Dewey in Hong Kong, driving the first automobile seen in Denmark, and photographing a mighty eruption of Vesuvius.

In 1918, wearing a war correspondent's uniform, he shot army scenes on the Western Front and his films surpassed those of the poorly organized newsreel cameramen. In 1923, flying for the first time, he had his most dangerous experience, when his plane almost crashed between Toulouse and Rabat. Later, in

Berlin, he found his dollar worth ten million marks, and in Africa he interviewed Emperor Haile Selassie in French, and, closer to home, he flew 20,000 miles over Central and South America.

Burton Holmes enjoys company on his trips. By coincidence, they are often celebrities. Holmes traveled through Austria with Maria Jeritza, through Greece with E.F. Benson, through the Philippines with Dr. Victor Heiser. He covered World War I with Harry Franck, wandered about Japan with Lafcadio Hearn's son, crossed Ethiopia with the Duke of Gloucester. He saw Hollywood with Mary Pickford, Red Square with Alma Gluck, and the Andes with John McCutcheon.

Of the hundreds of travelogues that Holmes has delivered, the most popular was "The Panama Canal." He offered this in 1912, when the "big ditch" was under construction, and news-hungry citizens flocked to hear him. Among less timely subjects, his most popular was the standard masterpiece on Oberammergau, followed closely by his illustrated lectures on the "Frivolities of Paris," the "Canals of Venice," the "Countryside of England" and, more currently, "Adventures in Mexico." Burton Holmes admits that his greatest failure was an elaborate travelogue on Siam, even though it seemed to have everything except Anna and the King thereof. Other failures included travelogues on India, Burma, Ethiopia, and—curiously—exotic Bali. The only two domestic subjects to fizzle were "Down in Dixie" in 1915 and "The Century of Progress Exposition" in 1932.

All in all, the success of Holmes's subjects has been so consistently high that he has never suffered seriously from competition. One rival died, another retired eight years ago. "I'm the lone survivor of the magic-lantern boys," says Holmes. Of the younger crowd, Holmes thought that Richard Halliburton might become his successor. "He deserved to carry the banner," says Holmes. "He was good-looking, with a fine classical background, intelligent, interesting, and he really did those darn-fool stunts." Halliburton, who had climbed the Matterhorn, swum the Hellespont, followed the Cortés train through Mexico, lectured with slides. "I told him to throw away the slides," says Holmes. "He was better without them, his speech was so colorful." When Halliburton died attempting to sail a Chinese junk across the Pacific, Holmes decided to present an illustrated lecture on "The Romantic Adventures of Richard Halliburton." He used his own movies but, in the accompanying talk, Halliburton's written text. "It was a crashing failure," sighs Holmes. "His millions of fans did not want to hear me, and my fans did not want to know about him."

For a while, Hollywood appeared to be the travelogue's greatest threat. Holmes defeated this menace by marriage with the studios. He signed a contract with Paramount, made fifty-two travel shorts each year, between 1915 and 1921. Then, with the advent of talking pictures, Holmes joined Metro-Goldwyn-Mayer and made a series of travelogues, released in English, French, Italian, Spanish. In 1933, he made his debut in radio, and in 1944 made his first appearance on television.

Today, safe in the knowledge that he is an institution, Holmes spends more and more time in his rambling, plantation-style, wooden home, called "Topside," located on a hill a mile above crowded Hollywood Boulevard. This dozen-roomed brown house, once a riding club for silent day film stars, and owned for six years by Francis X. Bushman (who gave it Hollywood's first swimming pool, where Holmes now permits neighborhood children to splash), was purchased by Holmes in 1930. "I had that M-G-M contract," he says, "and it earned me a couple of hundred thousand dollars. Well, everyone with a studio contract immediately gets himself a big car, a big house, and a small blonde. I acquired the car, the house, but kept the blonde a mental acquisition." For years, Holmes also owned a Manhattan duplex decorated with costly Japanese and Buddhist treasures, which he called "Nirvana." Before Pearl Harbor, Holmes sold the duplex, with its two-million-dollar collection of furnishings, to Robert Ripley, the cartoonist and oddity hunter.

Now, in his rare moments of leisure, Holmes likes to sit on the veranda of his Hollywood home and chat with his wife. Before he met her, he had been involved in one public romance. Gossips, everywhere, insisted that he might marry the fabulous Elsie de Wolfe, actress, millionaire decorator, friend of Oscar Wilde and Sarah Bernhardt, who later became Lady Mendl. Once, in Denver, Holmes recalls, a reporter asked him if he was engaged to Elsie de Wolfe. Holmes replied, curtly, No. That afternoon a banner headline proclaimed: BURTON HOLMES REFUSES TO MARRY ELSIE DE WOLFE!

Shortly afterward, during a photographic excursion, Holmes met Margaret Oliver who, suffering from deafness, had taken up still photography as an avocation. In 1914, following a moonlight proposal on a steamer's deck, he married Miss Oliver in New York City's St. Stephen's Episcopal Church, and took her to prosaic Atlantic City for the first few days of their honeymoon, then immediately embarked on a long trip abroad.

When his wife is out shopping, Holmes will stroll about his estate, study his fifty-four towering palm trees, return to the veranda for a highball, thumb through the *National Geographic,* play with his cats, or pick up a language textbook. He is on speaking terms with eight languages, including some of the Scandinavian, and is eager to learn more. He never reads travel books. "As Pierre Loti once remarked, 'I don't read. It might ruin my style,'" he explains.

He likes visitors, and he will startle them with allusions to his earlier contemporaries. "This lawn part reminds me of the one at which I met Emperor Meiji," he will say. Meiji, grandfather of Hirohito, opened Japan to Commodore Perry. When visitors ask for his travel advice, Holmes invariably tells them to see the Americas first. "Why go to Mont St. Michel?" he asks. "Have you seen Monticello?"

But when alone with his wife and co-workers on the veranda,

and the pressure of the new season is weeks away, he will loosen his blue dressing gown, inhale, then stare reflectively out over the sun-bathed city below.

"You know, this is the best," he will say softly, "looking down on this Los Angeles. It is heaven. I could sit here the rest of my life." Then, suddenly, he will add, "There is so much else to see and do. If only I could have another threescore years upon this planet. If only I could know the good earth better than I do."

Note: Irving Wallace (1916-1990) wrote this article on the occasion of Burton Holmes's 77th birthday. It was originally printed in *The Saturday Evening Post* May 10, 1947. Holmes retired the following year from presenting his travelogues in person. He died in 1958 at age 88. His autobiography, *The World is Mine,* was published in 1953.

Reprinted by permission of Mrs. Sylvia Wallace.

BURTON HOLMES

By Arthur M. Schlesinger, jr.

Burton Holmes!—forgotten today, but such a familiar name in America in the first half of the 20th century, a name then almost synonymous with dreams of foreign travel. In the era before television brought the big world into the households of America, it was Burton Holmes who brought the world to millions of Americans in crowded lecture halls, and did so indefatigably for 60 years. I still remember going with my mother in the 1920s to Symphony Hall in Boston, watching the brisk, compact man with a Vandyke beard show his films of Venice or Bali or Kyoto and describe foreign lands in engaging and affectionate commentary.

Burton Holmes invented the word "travelogue" in 1904. He embodied it for the rest of his life. He was born in Chicago in 1870 and made his first trip abroad at the age of 16. Taking a camera along on his second trip, he mounted his black-and-white negatives on slides and showed them to friends in the Chicago Camera Club. "To keep the show moving," he said later, "I wrote an account of my journey and read it, as the stereopticon man changed slides." He had discovered his métier. Soon he had his slides hand-colored and was in business as a professional lecturer. In time, as technology developed, slides gave way to moving pictures.

Holmes was a tireless traveler, forever ebullient and optimistic, uninterested in politics and poverty and the darker side of life, in love with beautiful scenery, historic monuments, picturesque customs, and challenging trips. He was there at the Athens Olympics in 1896, at the opening of the Trans-Siberian railway, at the Passion Play in Oberammergau. His popular lectures had such titles as "The Magic of Mexico," "The Canals of Venice," "The Glories and Frivolities of Paris." His illustrated travel books enthralled thousands of American families. He also filmed a series of travelogues—silent pictures for Paramount, talkies for Metro-Goldwyn-Mayer.

He wanted his fellow countrymen to rejoice in the wonders of the great globe. "I'm a Cook's tourist," he said, referring to the famous tours conducted by Thomas Cook and Sons, "reporting how pleasant it is in such and such a place." He knew that the world was less than perfect, but he thought the worst sufficiently documented, and his mission, as he saw it, was to bring people the best. Reflecting at the end of the Second World War on the mood of returning veterans, he said, "The atrocities and miseries will be difficult to forget. I know I can't give my Beautiful Italy lecture next session to men who know Italy only as a pigsty . . . One day these boys will forget and come to my lectures not to hoot but to relive the better moments and enjoy themselves."

When he retired in 1951, Burton Holmes had delivered over 8,000 lectures. By the time he died in 1958, television had taken over the job he had discharged so ardently for more than half a century. He taught generations of Americans about the great world beyond the seas. His books are still readable today and show new generations how their grandparents learned about a world that has since passed away but remains a fragrant memory.

THE WORLD 100 YEARS AGO

By Dr. Fred Israel

The generation that lived 100 years ago was the first to leave behind a comprehensive visual record. It was the camera that made this possible. The great photographers of the 1860s and 1870s took their unwieldy equipment to once-unimaginable places—from the backstreets of London to the homesteads of the American frontier; from tribal Africa to the temples of Japan. They photographed almost the entire world.

Burton Holmes (1870-1958) ranks among the pioneers who popularized photojournalism. He had an insatiable curiosity. "There was for me the fascination of magic in photography," Holmes wrote. "The word Kodak had not yet been coined. You could not press the button and let someone else do the rest. You had to do it all yourself and know what you were doing." Holmes combined his love of photography with a passion for travel. It didn't really matter where—only that it be exciting.

"Shut your eyes, tight!" said Holmes. "Imagine the sands of the Sahara, the temples of Japan, the beach at Waikiki, the fjords of Norway, the vastness of Panama, the great gates of Peking." It

THE WORLD 100 YEARS AGO 27

was this type of visual imagination that made Burton Holmes America's best known travel lecturer. By his 75th birthday, he had crossed the Atlantic Ocean 30 times and the Pacific 20, and he had gone around the world on six occasions. Variety magazine estimated that in his five-decade career, Holmes had delivered more than 8,000 lectures describing almost every corner of the earth.

Burton Holmes was born in Chicago on January 8, 1870. His privileged background contributed to his lifelong fascination with travel. When he was 16, his maternal grandmother took him on a three-month European trip, about which he later wrote:

> I still recall our first meal ashore, the delicious English sole served at the Adelphi Hotel [Liverpool] . . . Edinburgh thrilled me, but Paris! I would gladly have travelled third class or on a bike or on foot. Paris at last! I knew my Paris in advance. Had I not studied the maps and plans? I knew I could find my way to Notre Dame and to the Invalides without asking anyone which way to go. (The Eiffel Tower had not yet been built.) From a bus-top, I surveyed the boulevards—recognizing all the famous sights. Then for a panoramic survey of the city, I climbed the towers of Notre Dame, then the Tour St. Jacques, the Bastille Column, and finally the Arc De Triomphe, all in one long day. That evening, I was in Montmartre, where as yet there stood no great domed church of the Sacre Coeur. But at the base of the famous hill were the red windmill wings of the Moulin Rouge revolving in all their majesty. My French—school French—was pretty bad but it sufficed. Paris was the springtime of my life!

Holmes never lost his passion for travel nor his passion for capturing his observations on film. He has left us with a unique and remarkable record that helps us to visualize the world many decades ago.

Lecturing became Holmes's profession. In 1892-93 he toured Japan. He discovered that "it was my native land in some previous incarnation—and the most beautiful land I have known." Holmes had the idea of giving an illustrated lecture about Japan to an affluent Chicago audience:

> I had brought home a large number of Japanese cards such as are used in Japan for sending poems or New Year's greetings. They were about two inches by fourteen inches long. I had the idea that they would, by their odd shape, attract instant notice. So I had envelopes made for them, employing a Japanese artist to make a design.

Holmes sent about 2,000 invitations to the socially prominent whose addresses he took from the *Blue Book*. He "invited" them to two illustrated lectures at $1.50 each on "Japan—the Country and the Cities." ($1.50 was a high sum for the 1890s considering that the average worker earned about $1 per day.) Both performances sold out.

Burton Holmes's "Travelogues" (he began using the term in 1904) rapidly became part of American upper class societal life. Holmes engaged the best theater or concert hall for a week at a time. His appearance was an annual event at Carnegie Hall in New York, Symphony Hall in Boston, and Orchestra Hall in Chicago. His uncanny instinct for exciting programs invariably received rave reviews. Once he explained how he selected his photographic subjects:

> If I am walking through Brussels and see a dog cart or some other unimportant thing that is interesting enough for me to watch it, I am totally certain others would be interested in seeing a photograph of it.

A conservative man, Holmes avoided political upheavals, economic exploitation, and social conflicts in his travelogues. "When you discuss politics," he said, "you are sure to offend." Holmes focused on people, places, and customs. He offered his audience a world which was unfailingly tranquil and beautiful.

In 1897, Holmes introduced motion picture segments into his programs. ("Neapolitans Eating Spaghetti" was his first film clip.) His engaging personality contributed to his success. His crisp narrative was delivered in a pleasant and cultured tone. He always wore formal dress with striped pants before an audience. Holmes took pride in creating an atmosphere so that his listeners could imagine the "Magic of Mexico" or the "Frivolities of Paris." "My first ambition was to be a magician," he said. "And, I never departed from creating illusions. I have tried to create the illusion that we are going on a journey. By projecting the views, I tried to create the illusion we are looking through 'the window of travel' upon shifting scenes." Holmes's travelogues were immensely successful financially—and Holmes became one of history's most indefatigable travelers.

Holmes's lectures took place during the winter months between the 1890s and his retirement in the early 1950s. In between, he traveled—he crossed Morocco on horseback from oasis to oasis (1894); he was in the Philippines during the 1899 insurrection; in 1901, he traversed the Russian Empire, going from Moscow to Vladivostok in 43 days. He visited Yellowstone National Park (1896) before it had been fully mapped. He was always on the move, traveling to: Venice (1896); London (1897); Hawaii (1898); The Philippines (1899); Paris (1900); Russia, China, and Korea (1901-02); Madeira, Lisbon, Denmark, and Sweden (1902); Arizona, California, and Alaska (1903); Switzerland (1904); Russia and Japan (1905); Italy, Greece, Egypt, and Hong Kong (1906); Paris, Vienna, and Germany (1907); Japan (1908); Norway (1909); Germany and Austria (1910); Brazil, Argentina, and Peru (1911); Havana and Panama (1912); India and Burma (1913); the British Isles (1914); San Francisco (1915); Canada (1916); Australia and New Zealand (1917); Belgium and Germany (1919); Turkey and the Near East (1920); England (1921); China (1922); North Africa (1923); Italy (1924); Ceylon (1925); Holland (1926); France (1927); Spain (1928); London (1929); Ethiopia (1930); California (1931); Java (1932); Chicago (1933); the Soviet Union (1934); Normandy and Brittany (1935); South America (1936); South Africa (1937); Germany (1938).

Holmes's black and white photographs have extraordinary clarity. His sharp eye for the unusual ranks him as a truly outstanding photographer and chronicler of the world.

Holmes's lectures on the Panama Canal were his most popular—cities added extra sessions. For Holmes though, his favorite presentation was always Paris—"no city charms and fascinates us like the city by the Seine." He found Athens in the morning to be the most beautiful scene in the world—"with its pearl lights and purple-blue shadows and the Acropolis rising in mystic grandeur." Above all though, Japan remained his favorite land—"one can peel away layer after layer of the serene contentment which we mistake for expressionlessness and find new beauties and surprises beneath each." And Kyoto, once the capital, was the place he wanted most to revisit—and revisit. Holmes never completed a travelogue of New York City—"I am saving the biggest thing in the world for the last." At the time of his death in 1958 at age 88, Holmes had visited most of the world. He repeatedly told interviewers that he had lived an exciting and fulfilling life because he had accomplished his goal—to travel.

In a time before television, Burton Holmes was for many people "The Travelogue Man." He brought the glamour and excitement of foreign lands to Americans unable to go themselves. His successful career spanned the years from the Spanish-American War in 1898 to the Cold War of the 1950s—a period when Americans were increasingly curious about distant places and peoples. During this time period, travel was confined to a comparative handful of the privileged. Holmes published travelogues explaining foreign cultures and customs to the masses.

In this series of splendid travel accounts, Holmes unfolds before our eyes the beauties of foreign lands as they appeared almost a century ago. These volumes contain hundreds of photographs taken by Holmes. Through his narratives and illustrations we are transported in spirit to the most interesting countries and cities of the world.

Egypt

For Egypt, the 1860s were a time of progress in the Western sense. Egypt, more than any other part of the Ottoman Empire, had been drawn into the world market. The Egyptian government had modernized its administration, court system, and economy and had cooperated with the French in building the Suez Canal. Between 1861 and 1865, while the American South was unable to export new cotton, the annual export of Egyptian cotton soared. Extensive railroad construction took place. The Khedive, or Turkish viceroy, became a Western-type governor. The Khedive Ismail, for example, built a new opera house in Cairo, where in 1871, two years after the opening of the Suez Canal, Verdi's Aïda, written at the Khedive's request, was performed for the first time.

Such improvements cost a great deal of money. The Egyptian government was soon in severe financial difficulty. Nationalist protesters demanded that the foreign debt be nullified. Europeans had to flee Alexandria because of riots. In 1882, a British naval squadron bombarded the city in retaliation. British troops landed at Suez and Alexandria, and Egypt became a protectorate of Great Britain. The British government stated that military intervention would be temporary, but British troops remained there through two world wars and far into the 20th century.

Between 1882, the start of the British protectorate, and 1906, the year Burton Holmes visited Egypt, the British reconstructed the Egyptian economy. They reformed the taxation system, easing the burden on the peasants. They raised cotton productivity and encouraged the growth of raw materials needed by England. Of course, they guaranteed the regular payment of interest to European holders of Egyptian bonds.

Burton Holmes praised British "discipline" for rescuing Egypt from lawlessness and poverty. "Alexandria, once the greatest city of a classical age, had shrunk to the estate of a poor fishing village of five thousand souls. Today, Egypt is rich and prosperous and Alexandria a thriving and attractive city of more than 350,000 souls," Holmes wrote.

In this volume, Holmes describes the peoples of Egypt, their customs, and their traditions and included over 225 photographs. We join him as he explores Alexandria and visits the Egyptian antiquities along the Nile River. He describes out-of-the-way villages and their pleasant and industrious inhabitants. Many of the places Holmes toured and wrote about are gone—submerged under the Nile River when the Aswan Dam was built in the 1960s. Holmes has left us, therefore, an indispensable travel account of Egypt and its peoples almost 100 years ago.

CHEOPS AND THE SPHINX

EGYPT

TO go to Egypt is to go back to the beginning of human history. Beyond Egypt lies primeval mystery. The earliest pyramid marks the frontier between the unknown and the known, and in the wilderness of centuries that rolls between that pyramid and the oldest works of man in other lands, the only conspicuous milestones are the other pyramids, and the other Egyptian monuments that rise along the Nile. For more than a score of centuries the world was Egypt, and Egypt was the world.

A voyage up the Nile is like a thousand-mile mirage come true. In a mirage we seem to see wonderful things that we know to be impossible. Along the Nile we actually behold things that seem to be impossible because they are so wonderful. A mirage is only an optical illusion of wonders and beauty in the desert; but the river Nile has created a wonderful and beautiful reality, and that reality is Egypt, the ancient land that was the mother country of antiquity.

The valley of the Nile was the cradle of our civilization. In the sands of northeastern Africa the seeds of human greatness brought forth the earliest fruits of promise for our race. In Egypt, man first rose above the level of the brute. There, first, he began to cultivate the soil, to build cities, to establish governments, to write his story, and to commemorate his deeds in monuments of stone. In Egypt, Art, Letters, and History were born. For us, "the heirs of all ages," it is an inspiring privilege to visit this land of beginnings, this birthland of the genius of the human race. The Egypt of to-day is worthy of its magnificent traditions. The grandeur and the greatness of the past still are there, palpable in forms colossal, indestructible, and overpowering. And this Egypt of the fathomless past, this Egypt that was the mother of the

USERTESEN I, WHO RULED EGYPT FOUR THOUSAND YEARS AGO

world that we know, has called to us—children of the New World—across the centuries and across the seas, and we come obediently and gladly, for we owe her much in duty and in respect—much more in admiration and in wonder.

We who would read understandingly the world-book of travel must sooner or later not only read but study the great first chapter—the Genesis of history—the pages writ in hieroglyphs on the old papyrus manuscript that tells the Tale of Egypt.

The traveler must perforce visit Egypt backwards; he must begin with the picturesque Moslem Egypt of to-day and work his way slowly back into the far more significant and far more picturesque Pharaonic Egypt of unnumbered yesterdays.

England is now governing Egypt,—not directly, but through her masterly control of the native

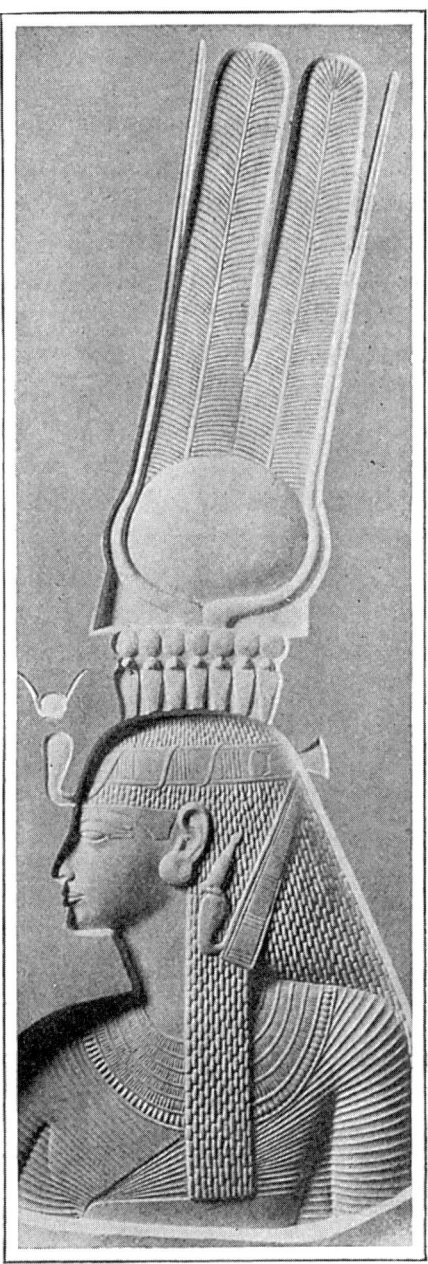

A KING'S DAUGHTER

organizations, political and military. His Highness the Khedive Abbas II Hilmi, born in 1874, has been the nominal ruler since the death of his father, the Khedive Tewfik, in 1892. He reigns by the grace of the Sublime Porte; he owes allegiance to the Sultan of Turkey; his nation pays tribute to the "Sick Man of Europe," who, by the way, now seems to be getting well; but as the guide-book politely puts it, "the Khedive's independence of action is controlled by the British plenipotentiary."

For more than a quarter of a century Lord Cromer served in Egypt as the British plenipotentiary. In his case the title was not a mere empty diplomatic phrase, as it is in the case of many an ambassador or minister. He was truly a plenipotentiary, endowed with full powers in the fullest sense of the word, and wisely did he use the enormous influence that his position carried with it, to the glory of Great Britain, and to the lasting benefit of Egypt. True, he labored in the interests of foreign holders of Egyptian bonds, but he labored like a statesman, a great man, and a good man. He has uplifted a downtrodden people and given them two things they needed most — water and justice. Cromer found Egypt worse than bankrupt; he made her credit good; he proved that honest government could be made to pay even in Egypt. He transformed a nation of slaves into a nation of freemen. The free Egyptian of to-day has learned to smile and is forgetting how

THE KHEDIVE ABBAS II HILMI

to cringe. The people who were ruled by the lash of their own rulers, whose fortunes and even lives might be taken at the whim of some official slave-driver, are ruled to-day with the strict but impartial rod of British discipline — and though now and then they kick against the pricks of law and order, they know that both their goods and their lives belong to them. They are learning in long slow lessons the new art of self-respect, and those who know enough to think without prejudice are grateful to Lord Cromer and to the nation that sent him hither and lent him the necessary force, moral and military, to establish order and to secure to them rights never enjoyed under the ancient dynasties of the Pharaohs or under the tyrannies of the medieval Pashas or of the Khedives of later times.

CROMER

England is not in Egypt "for her health," although many Englishmen do go there literally for their health, but she is there for the health of Egypt, physical, moral, and financial. England holds the keys of Egypt's gates and the keys of Egypt's treasury. The native may protest, and the modern Egyptian is a vigorous protestor, but the fact remains that Egypt belongs to England by virtue of the perpetual fiction of a temporary occupation. Egypt, before England came, was a land of lawlessness and pauperism. Alexandria, once the greatest city of a classic age, had shrunk to the estate of a poor fishing village of five thousand souls. To-day Egypt is rich and prosperous and Alexandria a thriving and attractive city of more than three hundred and fifty thousand souls.

LANDING AT ALEXANDRIA

To land in Alexandria at the height of the tourist season is to enjoy all the sensations of shipwreck, high-sea piracy, and war-time panic. Excited Arab porters in red fez and redder sweaters rush upon us, each eager to make a few piasters by making away with as much imported baggage as can be slung around him—each assuring everybody at the top of his lungs that he is the only real "Cook's man" in whole combination. "Want Cook?" "Here Cook." "Me Cook."

EGYPTIAN RED-CAPS

"Cook!" "Coo-oo-k!" "Coo-oo-ook!!!" They know that the infidel believes in Cook. They think that Cook is the god of the unbeliever, for the confused and befuddled newcomer always clutches at that word "Cook," as a drowning man grasps at a life-preserver. Meantime they clutch your cases, or anybody's, and piles of baggage melt away and disappear, we know not whither. We simply know that our belongings have vanished in a storm of talk. Egypt is the verbal storm center of the universe.

A VIGOROUS PROTEST

We find modern Alexandria an admirable city with little to recall her brilliant history, which reaches back to the golden days when the "Glory that was Greece" touched and transfigured for a time the fallen empire of the Pharaohs. The eye beholds no confirmation of the claims of the historians who tell us of an Alexandria which was as grand and noble in her marble splendor as in the intellectual vigor of her sons. Of all her architectural magnificence there now remains one solitary pillar, called Pompey's Pillar because it is *not* Pompey's. Even the date of its erection is not accurately known,

A MAN FROM COOK'S

but Dr. Botti, the curator of Alexandrine antiquities, assures us that this granite shaft, originally part of the vanished Temple of Seraphis, holiest shrine of pagan Alexandria, was reërected on its massive pedestal in the fourth century in honor of the Roman Emperor Theodosius, who overthrew the pagan

MODERN ALEXANDRIA

religion and established Christianity. We may say with reasonable certainty that this stone has been swept by the glance of all the famous eyes that ever flashed in Alexandria — the eyes of conquerors like Cæsar, Antony, and Pompey, of scientists and artists like Euclid and Apelles, and of fair women as unlike one another as the beautiful Cleopatra, slave of the senses, and the beautiful Hypatia, martyr to liberty of thought. But in all Alexandria there is no memorial to Alexander himself, unless it be the great city that still bears his name, or the lighthouse that marks the site of the colossal Pharos of antiquity, which was nearly six hundred feet in height and was regarded by the ancients as one of the Seven Wonders of the World. Remains of it were visible until about six hundred years ago. Then the sea swallowed its foundations and cleared the way for the erection of this

NOT POMPEY'S PILLAR

THE MODERN PHAROS

present tower, which is thus the direct successor of the classic Pharos that guided the Greek galleys and gave the name to every *phare* upon the coasts of France — to every *faro* of the Spanish main.

There are two routes from Alexandria to Cairo — one is the railway and the other the canal that brings the Nile boats down to the back door of Alexandria. We go by rail, first along the

THE RAILWAY STATION, CAIRO

banks of the canal and then across the wide, fertile reaches of rich delta land, past teeming towns of unromantic aspect, past miserable mud villages, over superb steel bridges, spanning the many spreading branches of the Nile, and at last, after one hundred and thirty miles of this new sort of monotony, our train thunders

PASSENGERS AND PORTERS

EGYPT

through a dilapidated suburb and rolls into the central station of the metropolis of Egypt. Metropolitan it well may be called, for Cairo has a population of nearly eight hundred thousand and is growing

THE CARRIAGE MEN

THE MANAGER'S "GLAD HAND"

THE CONCIERGE

larger every day. It is the largest city in all Africa. It is the capital of a now rich and prosperous nation numbering ten million souls, and it becomes, every winter, the Mecca of those cosmopolitan pilgrims of pleasure whose other sacred places are the Riviera,

ON SHEPHEARD'S TERRACE

GUARDIAN OF THE GARDEN

Palm Beach, Paris, London, and New York. Day after day, we see train after train roll into this Cairo station bringing the pleasure seekers and money-spenders of the world to Egypt's Capital.

We drive direct to Shepheard's, the original big caravansary for Christians in this Moslem city. There are now many other big hotels, some bigger, even more luxurious, but Shepheard's remains the heart and center of the foreign life of Cairo. The terrace of this hotel is one of the famous meeting-places for

TEA ON THE TERRACE AT SHEPHEARD'S

world-wanderers, a half-way halting-place in their race around the world. Not to know Shepheard's Terrace is a social crime. The traveler who has not trod the tile pavement of this terrace is little better than a stay-at-home, and the woman

THE OPERA AND IBRAHIM'S MONUMENT

of fashion who has not sipped tea at the tables on the terrace dares not look five o'clock in the face.

It is worth while to come to Egypt if only to indulge in the social joys of "the Cairo season," which begins in January and closes with the departure of the money-spending foreigners in early March. Meantime Cairo becomes a kind of Oriental Paris or sub-tropic London — with here and there pronounced suggestions of Atlantic City, Newport, and Longacre Square.

The modernization of Cairo was the work

"DOING" THE STRANGER

of the first of the Khedives, Ismail Pasha, a reckless but progressive despot who, catching the fever of civilization in Paris, returned with the resolve to transform his city by the Nile as Napoleon III had transformed the city by the Seine. The festivities organized on the occasion of the opening of the Suez Canal in 1869 cost Ismail more than twenty million dollars, and started Egypt on the road to ruin. His extravagances practically placed his realm in pawn. He built the Opera House of Cairo, where Verdi's "Aïda," written to his order, was produced in 1871. A statue of Ibrahim Pasha, father of Ismail, stands in the Opera Square, an offense to true believers, who, according to the Koran, hold it sinful to create the graven image of any living thing.

CAIRENE FACES

EGYPT

In this Europeanized quarter there are cafés on the sidewalks as in Paris, and we are often pestered by the Cairo prototype of the Parisian *camelot*, or peddler of petty and unusually useless merchandise. But in Cairo the hawkers hawk more kinds of merchandise than you will believe even should I read you a list of things offered me as I sat for half an hour at one of these cafés. I jotted down only the articles actually offered to me. I stopped at the fifty-seventh variety, for it was a mummied cat! The first thing on the list was a live parrot; then came such diverse articles as inlaid chairs, pistachio nuts, dried fish, red fezzes, Soudanese monkeys, post-cards, shimmering shawls, and an everlasting embroidered table cover held up to me a dozen times a day by an East Indian peddler, the most persistent nuisance

SMILES AND FROWNS

of them all. At first it is amusing, but in time it tries the temper of the traveler to be perpetually urged to buy things that no one wants and everybody buys, for buy we do, every purchase being the occasion for a gathering of curious onlookers. Every passer-by wants to enjoy the satisfaction of seeing the stranger taken in. Apparently the native eye revels in the sight of coin passing from hand to hand. Wherever money is paid out,

"BUY MUMMY NECKLACE?"

dozens of alien but interested eyes caress the silver or the gold as it gleams in the open palm. You pay your cabman; he immediately shows the money to the bystanding natives who rush up to see how much you have given him. You buy a necklace or an imitation scarab from one of the patriarchal dealers in brand new antiquities, and a group gathers to laugh at you if you have paid the price first asked, to compliment you with a look of deep respect if you have paid five cents instead of the five pounds demanded. The ups and downs of the stock market are nothing to the flights and falls of prices in this curio market on the Cairo curb. "How much?" I ask of the man who offers me some tempting trifle. "Six shillings," is the answer. "I'll give you six *millièmes*,"

ARE THEY BEAUTIFUL?

"BUY MY BIRD?"

I say, merely to escape the purchase of a thing I do not want, but all in vain, for though six *millièmes* represent less than three cents I get the goods.

But the real streets of Cairo are not found in the neighborhood of the hotel. We must plunge into the maze of the bazaars, reeking with color, before we can feel that we are in the real streets of the real Cairo — the Cairo of the Arabian conquerors of Egypt; it is as picturesque as any "Streets of Cairo" at an exposition. Everywhere there is strong appeal to eye and ear — and nose. We are in a world of novel sights and sounds — and smells. Tall minarets attract our gaze on high; loud-crying merchants call it down to the gay front of some dark, deep-set shop, one of the many thousand similar

IN THE REAL STREETS OF CAIRO

traps of temptation set for the tourist in these interminable bazaars. "To buy or not to buy?" that is the question with which the weak-willed stranger is everywhere confronted. His only safety is to lift his eyes again, and in his admiration for the ethereal beauty of those fairy towers of the mosques outlined against the pale blue of the sky of Africa forget the worldly lure of the curios of Cairo.

There are so many mosques in Cairo that the stranger fixes few of them in mind. The names of only one or two stand out; the rest will be remembered merely as fragile, wonderful, and in most cases dilapidated buildings of great beauty, which, though by no means abandoned, have an air of sad abandonment. One that will never be confounded with the others is the Mosque of

IN THE BAZAARS

El Azhar. It is the seat of the greatest of Mohammedan universities, the most famous educational institution of the Moslem World — a world which complacently believes itself to be the only world that is worthy of consideration. It is not generally known that the

TRAPS OF TEMPTATION

EGYPT

MUSHRABIYA

THE IDEALIZED ORIENT

Moslem belief is the most widely spread of all the religions of the earth, and though it seems to immobilize every nation that becomes Moslem — and Moslem or Muslim means "the submitted," those who are submissive to the will of Allah — it is itself ever spreading and ever increasing in power, though never progressing Its leading university in Cairo might be called a sanatorium where the half-dead sciences and wisdom of the Middle Ages are kept alive by all the arts of ignorance and bigotry. There are some seven thousand students daily in attendance; there are about two hundred teachers or lecturers on grammar, law, religion, science, mathematics, rhetoric, and poetry, but these Mohammedan professors are not permitted to teach or to know anything that is not vouched for and commended by the Koran. This, of course, excludes all modern science, all history, all accurate geography, — in fact, everything worth knowing. Absurd to the last degree is the curriculum of El Azhar, and pitiful it is to see seven thousand bright young minds being filed dull on the grindstone of the terrible Koran, to see seven thousand hungry souls asking the bread of knowledge and receiving only the stone of petrified tradition. This so-called university creates and fosters more ignorance and mental darkness than any other

UNIVERSITY MOSQUE OF EL AZHAR

institution in the world; and worse, it scatters its curse broadcast over all North Africa, and over Arabia, Turkey, Persia, the Moslem provinces of India, and all the Moslem lands and islands of the Orient. For all these countries send their most promising young men to commit intellectual suicide here in the halls and courts of El Azhar, where the students sit in circles on the floor repeating audibly the useless lessons set for them to learn — swaying their bodies to and fro as if in earnest effort to digest the lumps of petrified wisdom with which their starving minds are being fed.

MOSLEM "COLLEGE MEN"

In contrast to this studious roar of many voices is the calm quietude of other mosques devoted solely to prayer and to religious meditation. In every mosque we find the ornamental niche or *mihrab* set in the wall, marking the direction in which Mecca lies, so that the worshiper may always face the holy city when he prays. Beside it rises the *mimbar*, or the pulpit from which the Friday sermons are discoursed by the *imam*, or clergy. Friday is kept holy by the Moslems because it was Adam's birthday, and because Adam died also on Friday The six great prophets revered by them are Adam, Noah, Abraham, Moses, Jesus, and Mohammed. Each of these prophets is believed to have revealed a true religion; but as he who reveals last, reveals the best and truest faith, so the revelation of Mohammed supersedes all others as the true faith of the faithful.

STUDENTS FROM MANY MOSLEM LANDS

According to the Moslem doctrine, all who professed the Jewish faith, from the days of Moses to the coming of the Christ, were true believers; so also were those who followed Christ's teachings until Mohammed came. But all who do not accept the revelation and obey the teachings of Mohammed, the latest and the greatest of the prophets, are infidels, and have no hope of heaven. Superb indeed is the assurance of his followers — they know that they are right, that all other men are wrong.

As for the Moslem ideas of heaven, they are hopelessly material. Paradise is a place of luxury and ease, and the very meanest inhabitant is promised eighty thousand servants and seventy-two wives chosen from among the houri of heaven,

EGYPT

THE FOUNTAIN

THE LIWAN OR PRAYING PLACE

THE MIHRAB AND THE MIMBAR

besides the wives he had in this world — *if he desires to have the latter.* No old, unpopular wife is to be forced upon him in his new abode of bliss. Moreover, the wives that he will choose in Paradise will be tall as palm trees and as graceful. Adam and Eve, they say, were sixty feet tall; thus we have been shrinking ever since our fatal start in life. Every heaven dweller will possess a tent of pearls and emeralds, wherein three times every day, three hundred waiters will serve three hundred different dishes all at once, but — happy dispensation — the last morsel of each banquet will always be as grateful to the palate as the first. Wine, which is prohibited on earth, will be served in heaven in quantities unlimited, but — joyous miracle — enough will never be too much, too much will never be enough! We learned of several curious petty superstitions while visiting the famous Mosque of Amr, the oldest mosque in Cairo, built by the man who conquered Egypt in the name of the One God and of

A CURE FOR INDIGESTION

THE MOSQUE OF AMR IN OLD CAIRO

Mohammed his Prophet in the year 640, only eighteen years after the beginning of the Mohammedan era. Abandoned now, the Mosque of Amr is filled with worshipers only once a year, when the Khedive himself, his entire court, and a multitude of the

A PROOF OF PIETY

faithful come to pray amid the marble pillars. Then many try the efficacy of their prayers in a peculiar way, for he who cannot squeeze his body between a certain pair of pillars set very close together, can never squeeze his soul into the narrow portals of Mohammed's paradise. In one corner of this mosque we saw a woman licking with avidity a certain spot in the wall, worn concave by the touch of many tongues. She did not cease as we approached, but continued to rub her tongue upon the stone until the blood began to flow. Then she and her companion put on their veils and went away. "She thinks that she is cured," our guide remarked, "that is believed to be a cure for indigestion." They lick this stone with prayerful assiduity until the tongue is raw, then, as our skeptical companion said, "they *can't* eat too much and so, *of course*, they get well."

The congregation seen in the city mosques on Fridays consists of men,— no women, no Sunday bonnets, no mild flirtations, no hymn-book held in one big hand and one little one, none of the things that make church-going easier for us. The Moslem woman prays, if she prays at all, at home. The

CAIRO FROM THE TOWER OF A MOSQUE

FROM A MINARET

man, the master, is the one who attends public service and prays for blessings on his house. In solemn state he goes on Fridays to his favorite mosque, the representative and proxy of those who are dependent on him in this life. The traveler often hears the call to prayer, but rarely sees the caller, for the narrow streets seldom command a view of these tall towers. Therefore one day we lay in ambush for a *muezzin*. Bribing our way up to the shaky balcony of an old mosque, we waited patiently till the noon hour, enjoying the exquisite outlook. Two men had come up with us, but why one of them had climbed so high we could not understand, for he was blind and could not see the view. But presently the blind man, who is not dumb, opens his wide mouth and launches fervently the midday call to prayer; he is the *muezzin*, and the words that he intones are these:

THE MUEZZIN

THE CITY OF THE DEAD OUTSIDE THE GATES

"God is most great. I testify that there is no Deity but God. I testify that Mohammed is God's apostle. Come to prayer; come to security. God is most great. There is no Deity but God." To these, other words are added, differing at each of the five different hours of prayer. The calls are given at sunset, at nightfall, at daybreak, at noon, and at an hour midway between noon and nightfall.

THE GATE OF VICTORY

Far more effective to the eye than the mosques of the city proper are those that rise from the sandy solitudes a little way beyond the eastern gates of Cairo, where,

EGYPT

artistically aligned, we see the nine most graceful domes in all the realm of Saracenic architecture. These domes mark the tombs of the last dynasty of independent princes who ruled in Egypt down to the Turkish conquest in 1517. This was the dynasty of the Mameluke Sultans, founded in 1382 by a Circassian

TOMBS OF THE MAMELUKE SULTANS

slave. The first of these great master-slaves was Barkuk, builder of the grandest of these imposing tombs. Its domes and minarets are still intact, but its interior is all a wreck. The revenues that once supported this and the tomb-mosques of Barkuk's successors were long since confiscated by a later government. For many years each mausoleum was maintained as a sacred institution, its endowments administered by a staff of holy men and its

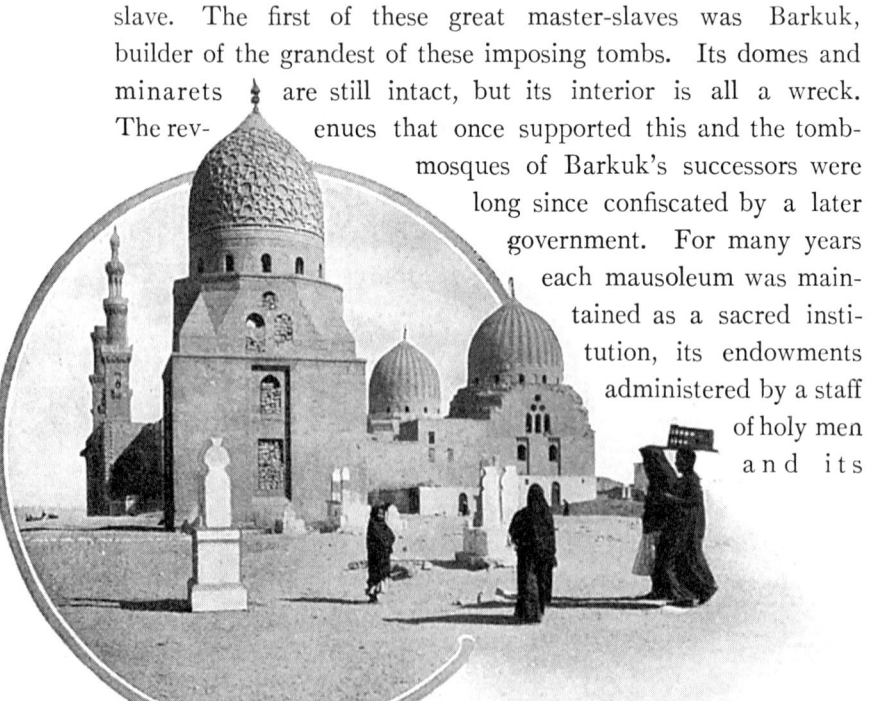

TOMB-MOSQUE OF SULTAN BARKUK

EGYPT

THE COURT OF THE MOSQUE

works of art cared for by a crowd of pensioners and servants. Splendid they must have been, these burial palaces here on the edge of the Arabian desert; splendid they are to-day, though crumbling fast despite the thoroughness of their construction. Five hundred years have not sufficed to mar the bold yet dainty pattern that adorns these domes, which look as if nets of curious design had been thrown over them, and at the touch been petrified. Thus the domes are apparently enmeshed in nets of chiseled stone.

Another day we make a longer excursion across the suburban sands of Cairo, riding forth from the gate called Bab en Nasr, the "Gate of Victory," on our way to the famous

A DECORATED DOME

forest of petrified trees, about eight miles from town. We reach the spot — a stone-strewn, sun-baked desert. "This is the forest," exclaims our guide, but we look in vain for trees. Scientists declare that the trees of this forest are extinct. This scientific pronouncement of a self-evident fact might be called a "work of supererogation" — the most unscientific mind grasps it at once. These are the most distinctly extinct trees on the face of the earth. On the ground, however, are fragments of what looks like wood, but feels like stone.

Our pockets filled with specimens, we gallop back toward Cairo to visit at the sunset hour the splendid Mosque of

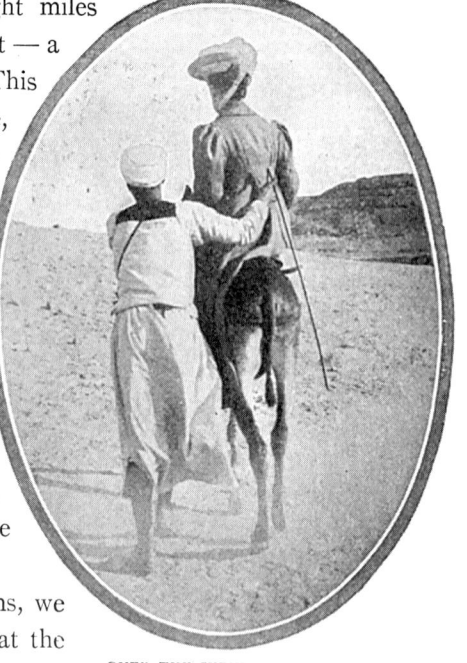

OVER THE SUBURBAN SANDS

THE PETRIFIED FOREST

Mohammed Ali, the dominating feature of the Egyptian capital. Its tall, slender minarets, and its low, graceful domes are seen even from the deep, narrow streets. It rises from the midst of the stronghold known as the Citadel, once the abode of Khalifs and Khedives. It is the crowning feature of the acropolis of Cairo. The builder of this temple was Mohammed Ali, founder of the ruling dynasty; he designed it as his tomb, and in one corner of it he lies buried. His was a strange career: born in Roumelia, he became colonel of the troops of the Turkish Sultan and was

THE CITADEL OF CAIRO

stationed in Egypt. Through French influence he was appointed Governor in 1805. Two years later he foiled an English attempt to get possession of the country, and in 1811 he performed his most sensational and brutal *coup d'état*. Napoleon had already defeated the Mamelukes and their followers, but the beys and princes of the Mameluke *régime* still possessed power and hindered the ambitious schemes of the new Governor. One day Mohammed Ali gave a great feast in the Citadel. Four hundred and eighty of the Mamelukes accepted his invitation. Superbly mounted, they rode up through a deep, steep passageway leading from the lower town. The cavalcade

THE COURT OF MOHAMMED ALI'S MOSQUE

IN THE ALABASTER MOSQUE

THE STRONGHOLD OF MOHAMMED ALI

THE HOLY CARPET CEREMONY
IN THE ROUMELEH

must have been very splendid for those beys were rich and filled with pride of race and pride of wealth. They had been forced grudgingly to acknowledge Mohammed Ali master of Egypt, they were about to break bread with him in sign of peace, and were content to wait until events should bring their party once more into power. But the man who was luring them to his stronghold waited for no events — he was a precipitator of history. His orders had been given. The lower gates were closed; the Mameluke cavaliers were caught in a trench-like

68 EGYPT

A "SAIS"

roadway; the armed men of the new master were behind the walls, through which or over which they fired almost point-blank into that mass of men and animals. The firing did not cease till all were dead, till every possibility of further Mameluke opposition was annihilated. Tradition says that one bold horseman did escape by leaping his Arab steed over a parapet, but after going carefully over all the ground, I must confess myself a skeptic on this point. But that nearly five hundred men were slaughtered there like cattle, this is history. Thereafter Mohammed Ali devoted himself religiously to the welfare of his people — as that sort of thing is understood in Oriental despotisms. An English student of affairs in Egypt, writing of the condition of the masses in 1834,

THE MAHMAL

EGYPT

A DERVISH CHIEF AND HIS ESCORT

declared "they could not suffer more and live." Yet they have suffered more and lived to see their land redeemed from poverty, if not from ignorance, under the business management of Englishmen. That the Cairene Egyptians are now prosperous seemed obvious on the occasion of the departure of the annual pilgrimage to Mecca. The crowds are well dressed and very well behaved, more patient than European crowds, as they wait to see the Holy Carpet started on its long and sacred journey to the holy cities of Arabia,— to Mecca, whence the prophet fled, and to Medina, whither he fled and where he now sleeps in his tomb. The most conspicuous feature of the procession is a fantastical construction called the Mahmal, which is carried by the finest camel in all Africa. Once upon a time the ruler of Egypt made the pilgrimage to Mecca riding in a splendid canopied throne on camel-back. Later rulers stayed at home and sent the royal camel and an empty throne. This "proxy" came to be called the Mahmal

AN AFRICAN SAINT

ONE OF THE ESCORT

and now goes every year to Mecca. The Khedive and his court witness the ceremony of departure from the great square called Roumeleh under the shadow of the Citadel The Mahmal and its escort circle three times in the center of the square, then move off in procession through the native town. We raced in our camera-laden cab through that maze of alleys, trying to get ahead of the procession, but by mistake turned into the wrong street and found ourselves mixed up with it in such a way that we could not escape, for the crowds closed in and completely blocked the side streets. We had to drive on slowly

THE SPECIAL CAR FOR THE TRANSPORT OF THE MAHMAL

THE NILE BRIDGE

with that sacred *cortége* — our presence in it being sacrilegious, the Moslem crowds voiced their indignation in cries we did not understand and hisses that we did. "What do they say?" we asked our frightened guide, "are they insulting us?" "No, not *quite* so, but they make *rough* talk." We were too

THE CAMELS IN THE FOG AT SUNRISE

much interested to be alarmed. The whole thing was so strange and wild that it was worth the risk, and on we went, the most observed part of the show. Sometimes we would be overtaken by the escort of some very holy sheik of some very holy society of dervishes. He would be swept past us amid a swaying of

THE NEW NATIONAL MUSEUM

green banners, on a wave of frantic and fanatical excitement. At moments like this, happily for us, the crowd would be so filled with religious frenzy that the one cab-load of Christian interlopers was forgotten. At last we reached the wider streets where native policemen are stationed, keeping the people back by means that are effective if not gentle. A bamboo stick across the bare shins of the Cairo rabble does wonders in the way of keeping them in line. Sound, whacking blows are struck on shins or backs, and sometimes heads are battered with the same bamboo. But there is no remonstrance; this sort of thing is mild

EGYPT

IN THE MUSEUM

and playful to a people who so recently were treated daily to the bastinado.

Formerly the pilgrimage was made all the way by land, the pious thousands traveling in caravan across the Isthmus of Suez, but now even the Holy Carpet and the

THE OLDEST WORK OF ART IN WOOD
"SHEIK OF THE VILLAGE"

Mahmal go part way by rail, part way by sea, and then by camel from Jeddah up to Mecca and Medina.

But all this has to do with the Egypt of to-day. Yet to see the Egypt of yesterday we need not even leave this modern Cairo — we simply make our way to the finest modern building in Cairo, the new National Museum which contains the priceless collection of Egyptian antiquities belonging to the government. In this museum we find ourselves in the realm of the art, the history, and the religion of the ancients — a realm too vast for the mere traveler, unless he comes prepared to spend many months — or even years — in the study of the fascinating science of Egyptology. We come to visit Egypt, not to study it, but in the simple seeing of sights we may learn much that will be better remembered than if it came to us in the form of lessons. In this museum a dead antiquity lives again — we see the men, the women, and even the domestic animals perfectly portrayed in contemporary statues of marble, stone, and wood, or what is still more wonderful and more uncanny, perfectly preserved in the flesh, the mummied corpses of those creatures of an age so fearfully remote, exposed to the eyes of our modern generation. Among the many

ONE OF THE SCRIBES

wonders that greet us in these halls there is not one that tends to make the old Egyptians seem more real to us than the famous wooden statue of the so-called Sheik of the Village. It is one of the oldest works of art in the world, carved about

TOILERS OF ANTIQUITY

TWO VERY HUMAN BEINGS OF THE PAST

five thousand years ago, and one of the most perfect. But it is remarkable less for its artistic worth than for its convincing fidelity to nature; we feel that it is a perfect likeness of the man it represents,— a very stolid, rather fattish, very human man, the prototype of many of the men we meet in our own streets from day to day. The original of this wooden masterpiece was, so they tell us, a nobleman of low degree, a rich and prosperous personage

DEAD MEN WHO DO TELL TALES

who, like the other wealthy men of his time, had a portrait-statue of himself executed, graven exactly in his own image, to be placed with him in his tomb, so that should his embalmed body fail to

FACE TO FACE WITH RAMESES THE GREAT

EGYPT

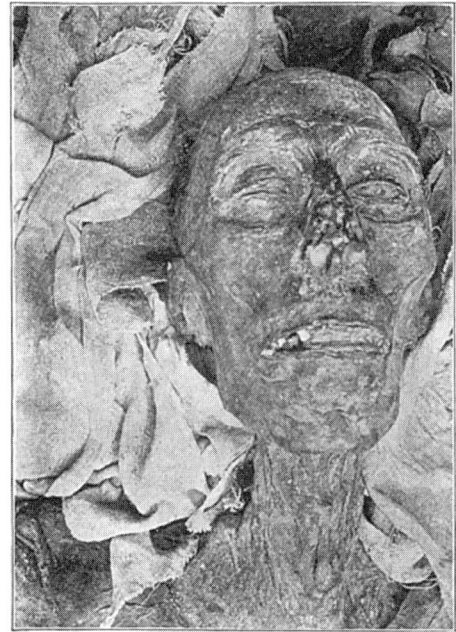

THE FACE OF RAMESES II

outlast the ages, his soul could find an appropriate envelope, and thus continue to exist and to enjoy. The old Egyptian believed that without a body, the soul or spirit must perish. Hence the hosts of mortuary statues, duplicates, understudies, *alter egos* that have been unearthed in Egypt; hence the attention devoted to the perfecting of the uncanny embalming art which has preserved for us through all this awful lapse of centuries the actual corpses of the kings and nobles of the ancient dynasties, the actual flesh and skin and bones of the Egyptian upper ten, the corporeal selves of the individuals who made Egyptian history. Think of the wonder of it! Here in this superb modern museum we may meet the ancient kings of Egypt, see the actual bodies of the Pharaohs, look upon the great Rameses face to face! Here he lies, marked "Exhibit J," his

THE FACE OF SETI I

royal body all unwrapped, his royal limbs exposed. His royal face, that hawk-like face of Egypt's master, the face before the frown of which all Egypt trembled more than three thousand years ago, is bared to the gaze of the meanest of his people, to the stares of every flippant foreign passerby We see the nose — a conqueror's nose — a nose like that of Alexander or Wellington; we see the mouth — a master's mouth — firm set like that of Cæsar or Napoleon, and in it there still gleams one solitary tooth. When the royal form was first unwrapped a ghastly thing occurred. As the countless mummy bandages were unrolled by the painstaking archeologists, suddenly, silently, but surely and visibly, Rameses the Great raised up his hand, as if to protest against this profanation of his kingly mummy, or to salute the scientists who had resurrected him. Of course the startling movement was caused by the expansion or contraction of certain tissues freed by the removal of the tight wrappings of the mummy shroud in which the body had been rolled three thousand one hundred and six years before. Then, turning to another case — which has become a royal casket — we peer down at the face of Rameses' father, Seti the First. He was the builder of the most exquisite, if not the

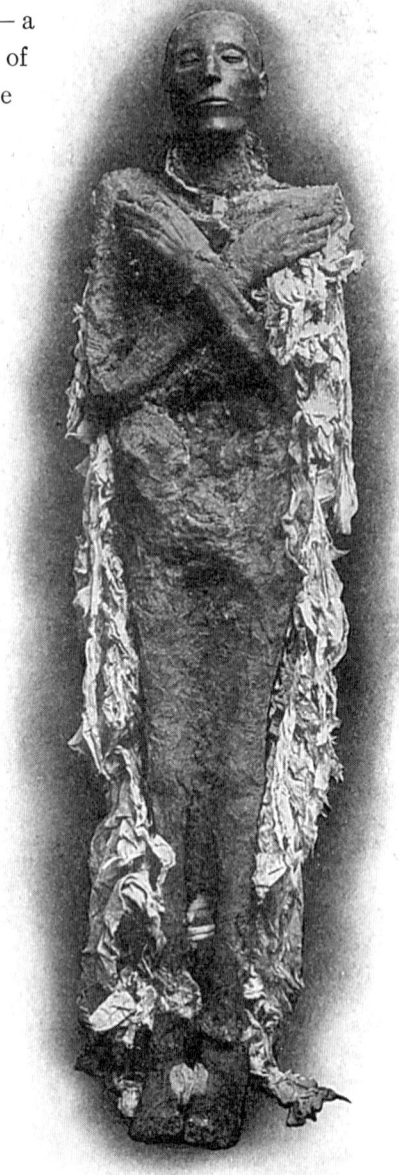

SETI THE FATHER

biggest, of old Egypt's monuments. His coffin was the most wonderful sarcophagus ever found in Egypt, a colossal block of alabaster superbly adorned with exquisite reliefs. You may see it now in London, in the Soane Museum, near Lincoln's Inn. In his day the embalming art reached a perfection never attained by the embalmers of earlier or later periods. His mummy is therefore better preserved than those of his predecessors or successors. Comparing the face of Seti with that of his more renowned and more ambitious son, we see that it is nobler than the face of Rameses, but less masterful. Seti it was who sowed the seeds of greatness. Rameses it was who reaped the harvest of world-wide renown. And what an experience, thus to compare, not the likenesses, but the actual bodies of two great historical characters, the father who died comparatively young, side by side with the son, whose body was the garment of his soul for more than ninety years. Yet here they are, the father a young and very handsome man, the son a decrepit nonagenarian, worn to a skeleton by more than three-score years of absolute imperial power. And think of it, these men were wrapped up in these very shrouds nearly a thousand years before the age of Alexander. And in this same hall lie other royal mummies, Pharaohs of three great dynasties. Great even among

RAMESES THE SON

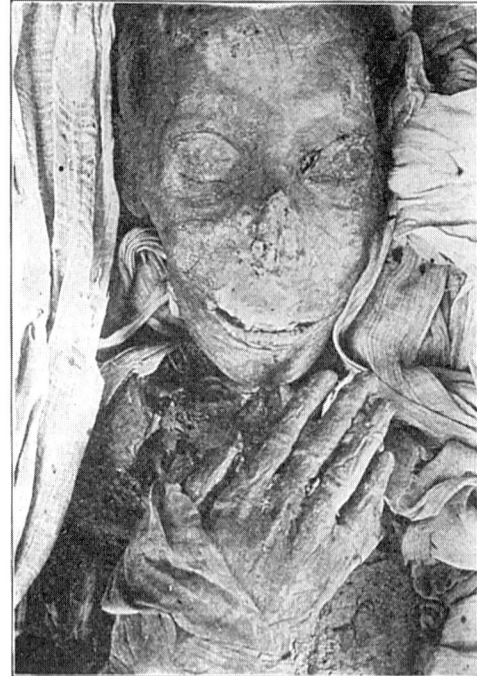

THOTMES III

the greatest of these kings was Thotmes III, who ruled two hundred years before the days of Rameses. He was the Alexander of old Egypt, for he made himself, through many successful campaigns, lord over every country in the known world. He it was who inscribed on the walls of Karnak the list of six hundred and twenty-eight nations vanquished and cities captured by his victorious armies. At ancient Heliopolis, the site of which lies near that of modern Cairo, he erected obelisks to commemorate his many jubilees. They stood before the gates of the great temples that once marked the intellectual center of the world to which came the wise men of all countries, among them Moses, Pythagoras, and Euclid, seeking the wisdom of the priests of Heliopolis. Plato himself studied for thirteen years under the tutelage of the priests of Ammon, whose sanctuary was the

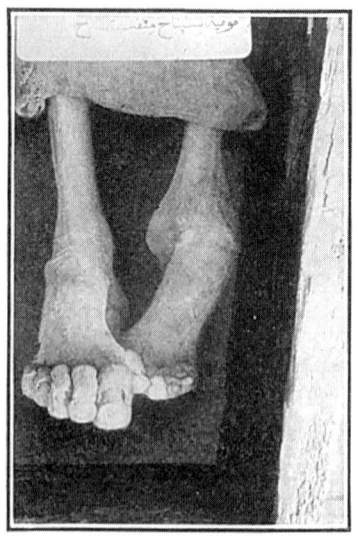

THE FEET OF A PHARAOH

EGYPT

earliest of all universities. Vanished are the temples, gone are all the obelisks save one, — gone but not vanished, for three of the former companions of this now solitary shaft stand to-day, each in the heart of a great modern city. One we have seen in London, beside the river Thames, the oldest object of all London,

HELIOPOLIS

making the British metropolis seem almost new; another stands in Central Park, in the great playground of the newest of great cities; a third tall granite monolith from Heliopolis rises in Rome before the greatest church of Christendom, St. Peter's. Other obelisks grace other sites in Rome and in Constantinople; but here at Heliopolis, where they first rose as everlasting monuments to royal pride, there is now only one. *Sic transit gloria mundi.* So passes the glory of the world. Will the site of London, New York, or Rome ever come to desolation such as this? Yet here was once a city famous for the things that do not die — religion and philosophy.

Yet how impressive is this lonely obelisk of Heliopolis, how eloquent of the grandeur of the past! How comparatively inconsequential seems the modern Moslem Egypt which has risen on the ruins of the ancient Egypt of the Pharaohs! Literally, the greater buildings of modern Cairo have been constructed with stones stolen from the structures of the ancients, and yet the greatest of these ancient structures which rise on the edge of the Libyan desert, about six miles from Cairo on the west bank of the Nile, do not at first glance betray the fact that they have suffered from this vandalism.

Man made, but man cannot destroy, the Pyramids. The Pyramids are destined to perish only with the world. "All things fear Time, but Time fears the Pyramids." Never to be forgotten is the moment when we first behold the outlines of those solid

THE PYRAMIDS

shapes, gigantic and triangular, that stand for all the glory and the dignity of the Egypt of the past. We murmur, "The Pyramids!" That is all that should be said: "The Pyramids!" All history is breathed in that one word, the story of our race from to-day back to the dim beginning. Who looks upon the Pyramids for the first

THE ROYAL CEMETERY IN THE SANDS

time keeps silence; they represent terrestrial Eternity, they almost paralyze imagination, because they alone of all the works of man bid fair to conquer Time. But what are the Pyramids? They are simply tombs — the burial vaults of kings who reigned about two thousand years before the days of Rameses, or nearly fifty centuries ago.

They are the hugest, costliest, cruelest tombs the world has ever seen. Eloquent of the wealth and power of those kings, they represent the suffering, pain, and toil of dumb, uncounted multi-

THE GREAT PYRAMID OF CHEOPS

tudes of slaves. They are the most flagrant, awesome symbols of man's inhumanity to man ever set up by pride and selfishness. And think of it, they mark the dawn of what is known as Civilization. Thus they have stood, an arrogant example to the proud and powerful ever since human history began. The first and greatest pyramid of this group, the pyramid of Cheops, was originally four hundred and eighty-one feet high; its base covers an area of thirteen acres, and each side measures seven hundred and fifty-five feet. So accurate was the work of ancient engineers that modern experts, testing it with the most delicate of modern instruments, have been able to discover only an error of $\frac{65}{100}$ of an inch in the length of the sides of the base, and of $\frac{1}{300}$ of a degree

EGYPT

in angle at the corners. Thus the pyramid was practically perfect, and, moreover, perfectly oriented in relation to the four points of the compass. It contains two million three hundred thousand blocks of limestone of an average weight of two and a half tons, and these were set together with a perfection of adjustment surpassing in *finesse* the work of an artist in mosaic. One hundred thousand men labored for twenty years to complete this tomb wherein the body of their king might rest forever in absolute security. But how vain his hopes of

FROM THE HOTEL VERANDA

THE TOMB CHAMBER OF CHEOPS

bodily immortality, how vain the efforts of his architects and engineers, the toil and drudgery of his workmen and his slaves. To-day the tomb is empty. The grave robbers of antiquity rifled it ages ago. They took away the treasure and doubtless scattered Cheop's royal dust to the desert winds. To-day we find there in the heart of the strongest, most durable mausoleum ever erected — in the tomb-chamber the most cleverly and trickily concealed—only the empty coffin that we see, only the bare granite walls upon which several generations of distinguished fools have scrawled their modern names. The granite blocks that form these walls weigh from forty to fifty tons apiece. You cannot conceive of the immensity of the Great Pyramid been boosted up hauled down the of this stone with hands — of masonry, this

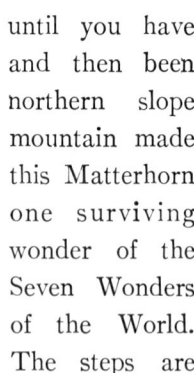

until you have and then been northern slope mountain made this Matterhorn one surviving wonder of the Seven Wonders of the World. The steps are narrow, barely fifteen inches wide; and to make matters worse for us, these steps are very high, about three feet.

CLIMBING A MATTERHORN OF MASONRY 451 FEET HIGH

EGYPT

Each step is just a trifle higher than the average leg and knee can manage. Hence the prosperity of that wild tribe of pyramid Arabs, the white-robed haulers and boosters who chaperon the traveler up and down for a fixed fee and all the *backsheesh* they can wheedle out of him. Climbing Cheops marks one of the big moments in the life of a traveler. That moment has now come for us. No wonder that we wear a look of tired triumph as we stand for the first time upon this artificial mountain-peak, older than many of the real mountains of the world. From the top of the Great Pyramid of Cheops, which, owing to the removal of the blocks that formed the apex, is now a level platform some thirty-six feet square, we look down upon the Second Pyramid, the tomb of King Kephren, about whom we know little save that he built the second largest pyramid. It is a curious fact that Kephren's pyramid, viewed from the desert or the plain, looks higher and huger than the one on which we stand. This is owing to the fact that it stands on higher ground. It still retains its sharp and clean-cut apex, cased in

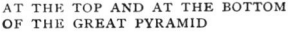

AT THE TOP AND AT THE BOTTOM OF THE GREAT PYRAMID

the smooth covering with which the entire structure was originally faced. Until the Arab Khalifs began to steal the outer blocks to build the mosques and palaces of Cairo, the pyramids presented smooth, sloping walls that were unscalable. But nearly all that facing has been torn away, leaving exposed rough stairways of unfinished limestone, save at the top of Kephren's pyramid, and at the bottom of the third and smaller one, where we find a few of the old outer blocks in place, showing us what the surface of the pyramids was like. Then, turning from these royal sepulchers we see emerging from the ever-moving tidal wave of sand that sweeps with the slow centuries around the triumphant pyramids, the head and shoulders of a thing that every member of civilized society, traveled or untraveled, knows by sight as well as name. Who does not know this face and

KEPHREN THE BUILDER OF THE SECOND PYRAMID

A LITTLE OF THE OUTER FACING STILL IN PLACE

EGYPT

"FATHER OF MYSTERY"

form, who need be told the name of the huge thing at which we are now gazing? Yet I have seen a guide — one of those loud specimens of cosmopolitan assurance — assemble his little band of tourists in this everlasting and world-famous presence, and pointing to it with a careless gesture, say: "Ladies and gentlemen, this is the Sphinx!" I almost expected yonder blind eyes to open and blast the miserable but earnest creature with a look. To-day, battered and broken by the attacks of Time and Man, this personification of mystery is flat-faced and featureless, its head the stony semblance of a human skull; but we feel sure that

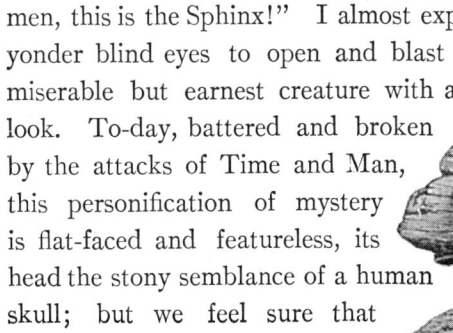

SPEECHLESS BUT ELOQUENT

A BURIED TEMPLE NEAR THE SPHINX

once this mutilated mask was beautiful. It is still wonderful. As Pierre Loti says, "It is still able to express by the smile of those closed lips the inanity of our most profound human conjectures." And thus the word "sphinx-like" will always be a synonym for that which holds but will not, while the world endures, disclose its mystery. We do not even know by whom this thing was made or when. We do know that it is cut from a ridge of natural rock, with patches of masonry added here and there to carry out the gigantic conception of the unknown sculptor. Here we should close our eyes and try to picture all these things as they were in the remote days when the Sphinx was perfect, when the Pyramids were intact and immaculate and loomed in all their geometric beauty as the dominating features of the grandest cemetery the world has ever seen.

WHERE KEPHREN'S STATUES WERE FOUND

EGYPT

THE SAKKARA SANDS

It was the cemetery of Memphis, metropolis of Egypt, housing the dead of many generations. To-day it is not possible to dig anywhere along this sandy plateau on the west side of the Nile without finding a tomb or *mastaba*. Mummies lie there as thick as cord-wood, and mortuary antiquities are unearthed in

THE STEP PYRAMID

RAMESES AT MEMPHIS

such quantities that the museum sells authentic "ushabti"—little figures representing servants, buried with the rich or noble — at five cents apiece.

Even such large things as pyramids are comparatively numerous. There are no fewer than seventy-six of them, rising in royal impressiveness from the

RAMESES WAS A HANDSOME MAN

sands under which hundreds of thousands of lesser stone-built or rock-cut tombs are buried. The oldest is the Step Pyramid, one of the group at Sakkara about twenty miles south of the more famous group at Gizeh.

The Step Pyramid of Sakkara is regarded as the oldest stone superstructure in the world. Between it and the Nile lay the great

BY THE RIVER OF RAMESES

city of Memphis, metropolis of King Menes, the first Egyptian monarch whose name is known to history, the founder of the earliest known dynasty in the year 3400 B. C. One of the two things that mark the site of vanished Memphis is a prostrate colossal image of the comparatively modern Rameses II. Egypt's vainest and most ostentatious king; the other is another similar colossal statue of the same noble old self-advertiser of antiquity. Rameses the Great was the originator of spectacular advertising. We shall find the results of his activity all over Egypt, but where the modern advertiser uses perishable paper Rameses employed imperishable stone. He left his mark on everything in Egypt except upon the shifting sands which have refused to perpetuate his fame as the digger of an embryo Suez Canal. He carved his likenesses on the eternal cliffs of the Nile or framed them between the pillars of the solidest of temples. He blazoned the story

NILE FELUCCAS

of his life and deeds upon the walls of giant pylons, that all posterity might look and read and marvel and applaud. The vanity of Rameses was as colossal as his memorials, that are so numerous and conspicuous as to lead the unread traveler to believe that Rameses was not only the greatest, but the *only* king that Egypt ever had. We shall see many of those reminders of Rameses as we go cruising up the Nile.

There are three usual ways of going up the Nile, by rail, by *dahabiyeh*, or by excursion steamer. To go up by rail is to miss absolutely the charm of the trip, to sail up in a *dahabiyeh* is very

LIKE THE WALLS OF THE ARIZONA CAÑON

costly both in money and in time, and therefore most people go by one of the tourist steamers that make the regular cruise up to the second cataract and back to Cairo in twenty-one days. We make our Nile cruise in the "*Nemo,*" a little steam yacht chartered for thirty-five days, and paid for by the thousands of kind fellow-travelers who do their traveling with us in the travelogues. The "*Nemo*" is manned by seventeen men. There is the captain, who is also chief-steward, a German; two waiters, Nubians; the chef and his assistant, Arabs; the engineer, a villain; the assistant engineer and stoker, so soiled that nationality did not

OUR STEAM YACHT, THE "NEMO"

show through the grime; four sailors, Nubian and native; a chief pilot, more like a monkey than a man; three other pilots picked up at various ports, and last, but never least, the Dragoman, Gattas George, a Coptic Christian and as kindly a soul as ever answered the questions of a tourist. Who and what are the Copts? They are native Egyptians; but though they wear the red fez of the Arab, and though their priests wear the round turban of the Turk, these Coptic Egyptians are not Mohammedans.

GATTAS GEORGE, DRAGOMAN

They represent the Christianized section of the native population. Their Christianity is almost as old as that of the Apostles, and since the fifth century they have had their own independent Coptic Church, which is dominant to day in

THE ACROPOLIS OF THE COPTS

COPTIC PRIESTS

Abyssinia. Their language is the old Egyptian language. The language that we see written in hieroglyphics on the obelisks and temples is the Coptic language, now written by the Copts in Grecian characters. But while they read it in their churches they rarely speak it, for in the affairs of daily life they use modern Arabic, the language of their Mohammedan neighbors, whose populous villages we pass at frequent intervals as we steam slowly southward against the yellow current of the Nile.

THE "BACKSHEESH CLUB"

A MUD VILLAGE

Some say the Nile voyage is monotonous, but one who loves color and pictures will never find it so. We are kept on the continual *qui vive* for the color effects which come and go with every passing hour and for fine compositions formed and framed in every passing mile. We never tire of the sailing boats that wing their silent way like butterflies along the golden pathway of the Nile. We like them best when they are coming toward us, or slipping straight away up or down the placid stream. The full face of a Nile *felucca* is always *distingué* and beautiful, but the profile is distinctly disappointing. Thus all depends on the point of view; head-on, the boats are fairy craft, graceful as gorgeous insects on the wing; on the quarter they have already lost their magical perfection of

AS IN THE ANCIENT DAYS

proportion, and when at last we overtake one and view it as it glides along abeam, the splendid argosy has become an ordinary scow, and the glorious, full-winged butterfly has grown as scrawny and as awkward as a humble sand-fly.

To our amazement we find many a mile of the river walled in on one side or the other by the high cliffs of rocky hills that rise upon the Libyan or the Arabian shores. The Nile boasts pali-

HIKING ALONG THE DIKE

sades surpassing those of the Hudson, and at time suggesting in form and coloring even the walls of the Grand Cañon of the Colorado. There is many a surprise in Egypt for the traveler who comes with notions fixed or preconceived. So, shattering preconceptions every day and every mile, we make our way with the aid of time and the tired engines of the "*Nemo*" against the current of the waters, but *with* the currents of the air, for

ON THE THREE WEEKS CRUISE

the prevailing winds are from the south. It is a curious fact that it is easy to sail up the Nile, but very difficult to sail down the river, for the winds are stronger than the current.

We are in the month of February and the Nile is getting lower every day. In October it overflowed these high banks and enriched the fields for miles in both directions with its waters — which in retiring left a mass of rich Abyssinian mud, the annual gift of the equatorial rains and the Abyssinian mountains to the thirsty, hungry valley of the Nile. To keep the fields and farms alive water must be kept upon them all the year, and to this one and all-important end, three fifths of Egypt's adult male population will labor every day and all day until the inundation comes again. Meantime the water must be literally lifted from the ebbing Nile and poured over the high banks to keep the farms and fields alive. There are two immemorial contrivances for lifting water still in use along this immemorial river. One is the *sakiyeh*, a wheel with an endless chain of pots, turned by a donkey, a bullock, or a camel — a primitive machine that is always in

A SAKIYEH

EGYPT

SHADUFS

motion and as audible as it is inharmonious. No one who has not heard the all-day, all-night song of the *sakiyeh* can realize how awful and uncanny a never-ending creak can be. The other watering device is the *shaduf*, a long well-sweep with a counterpoise of stone or hardened mud, worked by a pair of human animals in the form of swarthy, well-muscled *fellahin*. When the Nile is very low *shadufs* are arranged one above another, each pair of native dippers lifting the water to a level attainable by the dipping sacks of the *shaduf* next above. We see thousands of *shadufs* along the banks employing twice as many thousands of those bronzed athletes, whose splendid physical development

LIFTING THE WATER OF THE NILE

is due to this continuous gymnastic dipping exercise, and whose lives depend upon it,— for should the *shaduf* stop, the crops would die, the *fellahin* would starve, and so these men are literally dipping for dear life. Something of the inexorableness of Nature is brought home to us as we glide past those endless ranks of naked toilers bending their backs at the command of Nature's terrible

A SUGAR MILL

task-master, who bears the name Necessity! How poor they are. Everywhere the outstretched hand, the eager cry; on every lip the word that means a gift, for *backsheesh*, the first and last sigh of the Egyptian, is simply the Arabic word that means a "gift."

But all Egyptians are not beggars; only those at the ports where tourist steamers call. We found many a self-reliant community in the out-of-the-way villages at which we stopped. It was indeed a pleasure to meet a population that did not seem to know the word *backsheesh*. The *backsheesh* nuisance has been created and is fostered by the tourist; we who throw money to

COUNTLESS CARGOES OF CANE

be scrambled for are to blame for much of the beggary along the Nile. The Egyptian is naturally industrious; he has to be industrious to live. It astonishes the traveler to learn that Egypt is a crowded country, that in density of population Egypt surpasses Belgium, which has the densest population of any European country. But in computing the area of Egypt, the desert area is not counted; only the irrigated and productive area is considered, and this, of course, is comparatively small. Therefore it is not after all so

BULLOCK AND BUFFALO

strange that the narrow strips of fertile soil along the borders of the Nile should boast an agricultural population denser than the industrial population of overcrowded Belgium. The government is making magnificent efforts to enlarge the cultivable area of Egypt. Already millions of new acres, reclaimed from

THE CEMETERY OF ASSIUT

the desert by irrigation, are producing crops of cotton and of sugar-cane. The chimneys of great sugar-mills now rise like smoking obelisks where once the thirsty sands reached down and vainly tried to drink the life-giving water of the yellow Nile. Water has brought life and the possibility of wealth to the dying, starving native, and British justice now enables him to keep and to enjoy the wealth he earns.

In the old days no man dared to earn more than enough to satisfy his daily needs, for any surplus was sure to be a source of suffering. He would be forced by torture to give up his gold. Thus laziness became a secure virtue, and industry a dangerous vice. Now all that is being changed, with water as the saving agent, and canals, ditches, barrages, dams, and dykes, the symbols of the new prosperity. One of the greater dams is near

THE CITY OF ASSIUT

Assiut, the largest town of Upper Egypt, with a population of about fifty thousand. But Assiut has a suburb more populous than the city proper. It is the suburb of the dead, and as we look down upon it from the rock tombs on Libyan hills it appears larger and handsomer than the city of the living. The cemetery looks more like a real city than the living city of Assiut itself. Far to the left we see the yellow sands of the Sahara, for cemeteries are always on the border of the desert. No precious, fertile acres are ever set aside as dwelling-places for the dead; the living have too great need of all the cultivable land. Still there is verdure and beauty in this silent city; the date-palms, which give so much to the living, lend their shade and protection to the sleepers in the whitewashed tombs. It is a pious custom of the Moslems frequently to visit the abiding-places of their dead,

ON THE EVE OF THE FEAST

and there is one occasion when they come and camp for three days and nights beside the tombs of their departed relatives and friends. Some bring tents, others simply move into the little dome-like dwelling-houses that stand beside or above the family vault, a house in which the living visitors spend the three days of the great festival which partakes more of the character of a picnic than a pilgrimage, for there is much merrymaking and good cheer among the tombs. A market is established, cattle and sheep are driven in for slaughter, and the rich give meat and drink to all the poor who ask, and of the askers there are not a few. Meantime a lively sort of fair develops on the outskirts of the cemetery. Less attractive than the dome-like houses in the city of the dead are the cube-like houses in the city of the quick, for Assiut itself is built of sun-dried brick. Dull and dirty are its streets, duller and dirtier the pitiful young

AMONG THE TOMBS

children. The saddest sights in Egypt are the children, unwashed, with filth-encrusted eyes that are losing their brightness and possibly their sight because of silly superstition. Fear of the Evil or the Envious Eye prompts the Egyptian mother to neglect the personal appearance of her child. A pretty, well-groomed baby would be sure to attract the blighting influence of the Evil Eye. So even the well-to-do parent permits rags and dirt to diguise her child, as she imagines for its own protection. She believes it sinful to wash the inflamed eyes or brush the flies away. She believes that water is fatal to the sight; she believes flies to be the remedy for the disease, while in reality they are almost invariably the cause and aggravation of that opthalmia which is so prevalent that Egypt is the blindest nation in the world, a nation of near-sighted, one-eyed, or dead-

DOMES FOR THE LIVING BESIDE THE TOMBS OF THE DEAD

eyed victims of a disease born of filth, ignorance, and childish superstition.

In the bazaars of Assiut we are accosted in good English by intelligent small boys with clear eyes and clean faces who prove to be pupils in the American Mission School. Two of them scrape acquaintance by means of a request that sounds very strange in contrast to the usual cries for *backsheesh*. They say, "Please, sir, to give me an English book — I like to read an English book." The only book I had to spare was Herbert Spencer's "Essay on Education," which may or may not have met with the approval of the Presbyterian teachers responsible for the education of these lads. The pair who escorted us back to the yacht were choke-full of school-book information. When the elder one learned that we hailed from Chicago, he rattled off the following fire of facts: "Chicago is in the State of Illinois,

EGYPT

County of Cook, on the shores of Lake Michigan, population two millions, two hundred thousand; a celebrated center of the grain and meat industry of the United States of America," and the other one piped up: "George Washington was the Father of his Country. First in war, first in peace, and first in the hearts of his countrymen!"

Above Assiut the Nile grows shallower and the channels very intricate. We run aground three or four times a day, but usually manage to get off again by dint of vigorous poling. But one day our *rais*, or pilot, ran the *"Nemo"* high and dry on a deceptive bar which held us as firmly as those Siberian "perricatts," on which our Russian steamer "sat" so many days in the course of our voyage down the Amur River several years ago. This happened in the early morning. We woke to find the *"Nemo"*

IN ASSIUT

motionless and the crew wandering around in the river looking, or rather feeling, for the lost channel. No help in sight, the desert on one side, deserted fallow fields upon the other. In vain the efforts of our crew, who toil for hours waist deep in the chilly Nile. Meantime our engineer sends a small boat down to a distant village to tell the headman that we are in need of help, and, to insure immediate assistance, a lie is told, without our knowledge or consent. The sheik is given to understand that the stranded craft is the yacht of the Minister of Finance with high officials of the government on board! The sheik comes promptly, bringing twenty-seven men whom he has autocratically pressed into service. Fear of offending an official is still the sharpest spur to native effort. The day is not far past when any government official, from the Sultan down, had the right to call for the free labor of the people when and wherever he desired it.

HARD AGROUND This system of forced labor, called the *corvée*, has been abolished by the English, save in emergencies when labor is required on the dikes or the canals during the annual overflow of the Nile; but in doing forced labor at such a time the *fellah* is simply working for the preservation of his own and his neighbors' property. But remembering the stripes and punishments of an earlier *régime*, our salvage corps of twenty-seven shivering villagers toiled with chattering teeth and aching backs for five mortal hours without complaint, but not without noise, for they howled like demons as they lifted, pushed, and poled the "*Nemo*" off the bar. When at last we were safely floated, I asked the sheik to name the sum that he would regard as fair remuneration. He talked the matter over with his men, and they fixed the amount of the salvage payment at forty piasters. This may sound like a lordly sum to those who do not know that one piaster is worth about five cents! Thus, forty of them make two dollars in "real money." Two dollars, not for each man, but for that strenuous gang of twenty-seven sons of Egypt who had worked and yelled like madmen for five hours. When out of the fullness of our gratitude we paid them one Egyptian pound, about five dollars, they grinned with joy and showed their chattering teeth again as if to say "De-lighted!"

Thereafter we steamed more cautiously up the devious and ever-changing channels of the Nile, making long stops every day

SOME OF OUR TWENTY-SEVEN SAVIORS

in order to undertake shore excursions on donkey-back to the tombs, temples, or famous sites that are the real objects of our journey. To tell of all we saw and enjoyed, to describe all that instructed, entertained, or bored us in the course of our seven weeks of Nile cruising, would be to transform our travelogue into a comprehensive treatise on Egyptian art, history, and religion. If we

AT ABYDOS

would make progress up the Nile as travelers, we must beware of taking with us too much excess baggage in the form of erudition. But even though it be a dangerous thing, we must take with us a little knowledge, else we shall be blind to the meaning of the things we come to see. We should know, therefore, that when we dismount from the little donkeys that have carried us for more than eight picturesque miles, from a modern mud village that seemed to be melting into the Nile, to ancient temples that seemed to be fretting away under the influence of the sand-laden winds of the desert, that we have reached the site of one of the oldest cities Egypt ever knew — Abydos. One of the holiest places in all

EGYPT

Egypt it was also, for there at Abydos was entombed the head of the great Osiris — god of the underworld, deity of the dead.

To be buried near the tomb of Osiris was the pious wish of every Egyptian. The Necropolis of Abydos is of vast extent. The desert sands cover countless multitudes of mummies; other multitudes of embalmed ancients were brought hither to rest for a time in sacred soil. Millions of memorial tablets were sent hither to represent those whose bodies lay in far-off provinces, but whose souls yearned for some sort of association with the holy one whose head lay in Abydos, for this association was believed to bring its blessing in the other life. To-day we find a similar superstition in Japan, where thousands of bodies, hundreds of thousands of tablets, and millions of single bones have been carried by the pious to the

THE FOOLISH CAMEL . . .

. . . AND THE WISE ASS

mountain forests of Koya San that they may insure for the dead the blessing that flows from the sacred sepulcher of Kobo Daishi, the St. Paul of the Buddhism of Japan.

The finest of the two surviving temples of Osiris at Abydos was

EGYPT

SETI AND THE IBIS-HEADED GOD

begun by the great Seti and completed by Rameses the Great. It was a seven-fold sanctuary, wherein were worshiped not only Osiris, but also Isis his wife, Horus his son, the gods called Ptah, Harmachis, and Ammon, and the deified King himself, builder of the temple — for King Seti, after death, became a god. Seti was the builder of the most beautiful of the old Egyptian structures. But his creations being more beautiful, less colossal, were the more perishable. As structures they have suffered more from the destructive touch of Time — and yet Time has spared much of their exquisite decoration. In fact, we shall

TINTED RELIEFS AT ABYDOS

see few art works more perfectly preserved or fresher in coloring than the tinted reliefs upon the walls of Seti's temple at Abydos, and yet these shapes were fashioned, these colors were applied, more than three thousand years ago. The figures ranged in brilliant array along these walls represent the gods of Egypt in friendly converse with old Egypt's Kings. The gods have heads

RAMESES AND HIS SON ON THE WALLS AT ABYDOS

like those of birds and animals, and the Pharaohs turn toward them, always in profile, faces that are very human and full of kingly dignity. The hieroglyphics, also cut in low relief and highly colored, tell of the deeds of the Kings — their gifts to the gods and of the gods' regard for the Kings who reared these temples in their honor — briefly, all this is a record of a mutual admiration society, composed of the earthly rulers and celestial deities, thus proving that a certain modern ruler's "Ich und Gott" is but a modern's plagiarism.

On other walls we find a different kind of picture-writing. We see King Rameses trying to lasso a rampageous bull, while

Rameses' royal son gives the tail of the unhappy animal a very skilful and apparently painful twist, suggesting that *jiu-jitsu* was not unknown to the ancients. Here both the royal figures and the hieroglyphics of the royal record are not raised in relief, but deeply incised in the walls. There is no coloring,

WHERE PICNICS ARE PROFANATIONS

and the execution is comparatively crude, for this is work of a later period.

In a long corridor called the Hall of the Kings we may read — that is, if hieroglyphics are not worse than Greek to us — that wonderful, invaluable list of the Kings of Egypt, which proved such a priceless boon to the historians who were groping in Egyptian darkness as to dynasties and dates and the order of royal successions. There they found the names of all the rulers from King Menes, whose throne was at Memphis, to Seti the First,

EGYPT

A PILGRIM

whose capital was at Thebes. Between their reigns more than two thousand years elapsed, yet so wonderfully is the dead and buried past being revived and resurrected by the researches of the archeologists that we moderns now possess one piece of King Menes royal regalia — a golden bar, the oldest known piece of jewelry — and the actual body of King Seti, builder of this temple at Abydos, where at the hot noonday hour we perpetrate an impious picnic amid the sculptured columns of the hypostyle hall, through which the later Pharaohs were wont

DENDERA

to pass, bearing their offerings to the seven gods enshrined in the seven inner sanctuaries.

Another day, another temple claims our attention and wins our admiration, for the great shrine of Hathor at Dendera is one of the most satisfying sights in Egypt, at least to the casual trav-

THE HATHOR FACES

eler who, when he goes to much expense, trouble, and fatigue to see a sight, demands a sight that he can see with his ordinary eyes, not one upon which he must turn the eyes of erudition or imagination to make it look like anything worth while. Dendera is eminently seeable. It "jumps to the eyes," as the Frenchman would say. It looms in stony dignity and with a certain heavy architectural grace. It refuses to be confounded with other temples. The tourist may mix his Egyptian gods and merge his impressions of many temples, but Dendera stands out clearly defined on the

EGYPT

page of memory. For an Egyptian pile it is distressingly new, dating only from the first century B. C. It was dedicated to the Goddess Hathor, the Venus of the Nile mythology. You may distinguish faces of that Egyptian Aphrodite on the capitals of the huge columns — faces half obliterated and disfigured by the Mohammedan or Christian zealots of a later age. Entering the temple we find ourselves in the noblest, best proportioned

THE VESTIBULE OF DENDERA

hall of columns in all Egypt. Even the far-famed hall of Karnak is to me less impressive than this vestibule of Dendera. Though the sculptures are inferior to those of older temples, there is in Dendera a certain impressive and mysterious charm that other grander, better executed temples lack. Perhaps it is because the roof is still intact, keeping in that atmosphere of mystery which at Karnak or at Abydos has evaporated from the columned corridors that are now open to the sky. In ancient days the mystery

TOWARD THE SANCTUARY OF DENDERA

EGYPT

was thick indeed. These temples were not praying places for the people, they were mere fortresses of luxury and mystery obstinately held by the priesthoods, which at last became so powerful that they ruled Egypt by ruling Egypt's rulers through their superstitious fears.

The holy of holies was a dark "hidden secret chamber," an occult alcove in the midst of the temple, forbidden to all men save the Pharaoh. To-day we enter freely. There is nothing in it; it is void and empty as all the other organized mysteries which have deceived mankind in ancient or in modern times. Once let the honest light of day into the black holes of superstition and those who live and thrive upon the superstitious fears of simpler minds are soon bereft of all their power to oppress. The greatest of the gods of Egypt was the Sun God, whose name, Ammon, is said to signify "hidden" or "concealed." His cult was shrouded

LIGHT IN DARK PLACES

in mystery and his glory revealed in magnificence. His priesthoods tyrannized over King and people, and ultimately the chief priest of Ammon — who had long been more than King — became the Pharaoh in name as well as fact. Church and State became one, and the greatness of Egypt as a nation was at an end forever.

TEMPTATIONS FOR TOURISTS AT LUXOR

The grandest sanctuaries of the god of gods were at Thebes, the mighty city where the mighty Pharaohs had their capital for about two thousand years. To-day the tourist hotels of Luxor mark the site of ancient Thebes, and offer shelter to the thousands of strangers who every season ascend the Nile, four hundred and fifty miles from Cairo, to see what remains of the greatest of Egyptian cities, the first great monumental city of the world.

TWINS

The old Egyptian name for Thebes was Net, which means "The City," and it was indeed *the* city of the age in which it flourished. The Greeks gave to it — for no good reason — the name of Thebes, a name borne by several of their cities in Greece and Asia Minor. The modern name, Luxor, is a corruption of the Arabic "El Kusur," meaning "the castles." The

PAPYRUS PILLARS AT LUXOR

castles referred to are the many-columned courts of the abandoned temples within which little Mohammedan settlements grew from hamlets to villages, and ultimately spreading round about the ancient structures which they had filled half-way to the brim with the filth and rubbish of successive generations, these villages have formed the town of Luxor that we see to-day.

Amenophis III, a great King of the eighteenth dynasty, was the builder of the temple to which the name of Luxor has attached itself, and from which all the débris of Luxor has not yet been removed. Some Arab dwellings and a whitewashed mosque, squatting upon deep strata of débris, still partly obscure the plan of this amazing assemblage of columns, courts, and corridors. Where the enclosure has been cleared the splendid pillars rise in majesty and beauty from floors kept clean by the care of the department of antiquities. The lovely lotus flower and the papyrus of the Nile were the inspiration of the ancient architects who designed these columned sanctuaries. Imagine clustered papyrus stems of stone, crowned by stone buds, tall as the pillars of the Parthenon, more numerous, better preserved, and endowed with a peculiar natural grace that leads us to regard them not as architectural creations, but as colossal things of beauty that have sprung, in all their everlasting dignity, from the sacred soil of Net, the city of the Theban Kings.

COLUMNED AISLE OF AMENOPHIS III AT LUXOR

Yet even this huge colonnade, the finest in all Egypt, shrinks into comparative littleness when we turn and gaze up at the huge pillars of the columned aisle reared by the same royal builder, Amenophis, who did not hesitate to risk eclipsing his earlier creations by beginning other buildings on so vast a scale that he could not complete them. The fourteen columns of his projected but unfinished hypostyle hall are the most graceful existing columns of their size, forty-two feet in height, surpassing in beauty the only columns that surpass them in size — those of the hypostyle of Karnak. We pass along that impressive aisle, assuming instinctively a kingly manner as if to make our bearing harmonize with the impressive towers of grace that rise on either side. We reach the columned court that Rameses added to the ambitious scheme of the earlier King, instead of completing, as he should, the great hall conceived by Amenophis. But alas, the vanity and egotism of the Pharaohs and the hugeness of the design of this temple — or rather series of sanctuaries —

THE PORTAL OF THE PYLON, LUXOR

THE GREAT COURT OF RAMESES

prevented its ever being really finished. The empire fell and the Pharaohs lost their power before this colossal building scheme could be carried to completion. King after King labored upon it, spending enormous sums of gold and energy on its successive courts. Rameses did even more than his share when his turn came, for he was sure to leave his mark, not only on his own new works, but upon the works of all his royal pred-

THE WIFE OF RAMESES STANDS BESIDE HIM!

MATE TO THE PARISIAN OBELISK OF LUXOR

ecessors. In fact, he usually made himself so much at home, in effigy, in the temples of his fathers that their statues were crowded out by his colossal likenesses. To-day the shrines of Egypt are peopled almost exclusively by stone semblances of that royal egotist. But Rameses was not only a great King; he was a gallant husband, and he usually had a portrait of his wife carved in the same block of granite, and if you seek that ever-present portrait of his queen, you will be sure to find it — if you know just where to look and just how far a royal husband dared to go in sharing glory with his wife. A very tiny Mrs. Rameses stands proudly by her husband's side, her head not reaching quite to the knees of her colossal granite spouse.

Leaving the temple and the town of Luxor — a town of about twelve thousands souls, that is, if we may so far outrage Moslem prejudices as to attribute souls to the *women* of the place — we make our way to the insignificant village of Karnak, the name of which now stands for the most stupendous if not the most significant ruins in the world. The ruins of the temples of Ammon at Karnak are to other ruins what the Grand Cañon of Arizona is to other gorges or ravines; and looking at the columns of Karnak which might serve as foundations for the earth, and at the walls of Karnak which might be the ramparts of creation, there come to our dazed minds no words so fitting as the words used by Charles Higgins in trying to convey to those who had never looked upon that glorious scene in Arizona — that Titanic chasm of the Colorado — some concept of its glory. He spoke of that stupendous work of Nature as we may speak of Karnak, this stupendous work of man, as "A boding, terrible thing, unflinchingly real, yet spectral as a dream, eluding all sense of perspective or dimension, outstretching the faculty of measurement, overlapping the confines of definite apprehension . . . the beholder is at first unimpressed by any detail, he is overwhelmed by the *ensemble*."

A PORTAL AND A PYLON

Well might the Pharaohs have regarded this creation, upon which the Dynasties had labored for

EGYPT

eighteen hundred years, as "The Throne of the World." It would be useless to give figures, measurements, or dates,— such ponderous facts weigh down the balances of memory and most of them would slip off the tilted scales. One word gives us the magnitude of Karnak, another tells its age — the one word is "colossal," and the other is "antique." But these words must be raised to the highest power before using them in an attempt to dodge a description of this temple which is indescribable. Elsewhere we have found it possible where description falters to make you see the things which cannot be described, but here at Karnak even the camera cannot be depended upon. There are no comprehensive points of view, no satisfying perspectives. There is so little free space in the great hall. The columns stand too close together; each is so huge that it conceals the others, and in many places the space between has been filled in with earth and gravel as a precautionary measure. Karnak has begun to crumble. Eleven columns fell in 1899; those that remain erect must be banked up and supported during the work of restoration. There were a hundred and thirty-four of them, the

THE HUGEST COLUMNS ON EARTH

larger ones nearly twelve feet thick and sixty-nine feet high. Upon the capital of each a Roman centurion could have massed his hundred men. The lesser columns are larger than the largest that we saw at Luxor. They are not monolithic, but composed of many half-drums superimposed, and they are not fluted like

WRECK OF THE SECOND PYLON AT KARNAK

the columns of the Greeks, but covered with incised reliefs which once were bright with color. They look firm as the everlasting granite hills that mothered them, but though the heavy roof has long since disappeared, relieving them of its enormous weight, the cumulative burden of the ages is at last proving too heavy for the greatest columns the world has ever seen, just as it long since proved too heavy for the mighty pylons. Down came those wall-like towers centuries ago, transforming the once imposing gateways into heaps of stony débris like that which marks the

EGYPT 131

pathway of an avalanche. In fact, all Karnak resembles the litter caused by some landslide or avalanche, the stones of which have taken on imposing shapes, suggestive of huge architectural forms. The bigness of what we see escapes us. We cannot grasp the size of things, for all things at Karnak are on a scale so grand that grandeur becomes commonplace — one colossal object makes other colossal objects appear small. Nor can we grasp the one-time wealth and splendor of this shrine which is now but a heap of broken stones. The Kings, who, when they came to worship, had to cover nearly one third of a mile in going from the entrance to the inner end of Ammon's sanctuary, gave of their wealth and spoil a lion's share to the god to whom they here bowed down. Tribute from all the known world poured into the coffers of the priests. Rameses III gave of his prisoners

IN THE HYPOSTYLE HALL

of war, nearly ninety thousand slaves, to Ammon. In time the high priest of Ammon usurped the temporal throne, and the first servant of the god became the master of the masses. At one time fifteen per cent of all the wealth of Egypt belonged to

THE CAPITALS OF THE KARNAK COLUMNS

the priesthoods; they were the trusts of antiquity; they dealt in prayers and promises of joy to be fulfilled beyond the grave, and they found in this traffic a colossal profit; it yielded returns as stupendous as the temples which were the counting-houses of those sacred corporations. Around about this grave of Egypt's yesterday stretch the fertile fields that furnish food for the man and the beast of the Egypt of to-day. The buffalo browses and the *fellah* tills the soil where once great Rameses rode through the acclaiming streets

THE SPHINXES WITH RAMS' HEADS

EGYPT

of Thebes in his triumphal chariot on his return from some victorious invasion.

Thebes was a city of wide extant,— we may cross the Nile and ride for several miles toward the western mountains and yet not get beyond the limits of that biggest of the big cities of antiquity.

At the time of its greatest glory, Thebes covered vast areas on both sides of the Nile — the eastern shore being the site of the city of the living, the western shore that of the larger, grander, and more splendid city of the dead. The

THE COLOSSI OF MEMNON

old Egyptian always looked upon his tomb as his real home. His house was but a place of passing sojourn; his sepulcher was his eternal dwelling-place. The Pharaohs reared them splendid mortuary temples on this plain, and set in front of them gigantic portrait statues of themselves. Two of these colossi, portraits of Amenophis III, still indicate the site of his mortuary shrine. His tomb and the tombs of all the Kings who ruled in Thebes were subterranean palaces, hollowed in the foundations of a range of hills a few miles to the west; but there on the plain stood an array of temples that were the gorgeous, visible ante-chambers, each one corresponding to one of those mysterious, unseen tombs. These statues give us some idea of the scale on which those vanished temples were conceived. The

DER-EL-BAHRI

EGYPT

northernmost colossus is the one known as the Vocal Memnon—the one which used to speak and greet the rising sun; but whether the sounds that once came from the now dumb monster were caused by a priestly trick, or by the expanding or cracking of the stone as the sun's rays touched and warmed it after the chill of the night, has never been determined. In the background, set close against the reddish cliffs, we find the temple built by the one woman who succeeded in achieving greatness in that distant age. She was Queen

THE PAINTED HATHOR COW

Hatshepsut, the first distinguished woman in history, the first and only female Pharaoh. Her temple at Der el Bahri has proved a rich mine for the archeologists. It was not far from here that they found, in 1881, those mummies of the Kings — of Rameses and the rest — which we have seen in Cairo.

The monarchs who ruled in Thebes, knowing that even the greatest pyramids of their predecessors had failed to preserve their royal remains from profanation, resolved that their own mummies should be, not buried under colossal artificial mountains like the Pyramids, but hidden deep in the foundations of the everlasting hills. So they commanded their royal architects to dig and burrow, rather than to build. They tunneled into the cliffs, two hundred, three hundred, and in one case nearly

INTO THE VALLEY OF DEATH

EGYPT 137

AMONG THE TOMBS OF THE THEBAN KINGS

seven hundred feet, descending in some places by inclined and in others by vertical shafts nearly two hundred feet below the point of entrance, which was always carefully concealed. More than forty of those entrances have been discovered; more than forty underground burial palaces of the Theban Pharaohs have been cleared and carefully explored. They have found long corridors adorned with painted pictures, two and three thousand years of age, but bright and fresh as if they had been painted yesterday. They have found spacious ceremonial chambers — long suites of subterranean rooms, their walls alive with tinted illustrations of the royal lives lived by the men for whom these deep,

ENTRANCE TO A ROYAL TOMB

PORTAL OF A MORTUARY PALACE

eternal dwellings were devised. But they found here, as at the Pyramids, that the royal graves were empty. A few mummies were discovered in the side chambers, but they were not those of the Kings. The royal mummies of the mighty Pharaohs had been

IN THE TUNNEL OF A TOMB

taken away secretly, at the command of one of their weak successors, in the days when the empire was tottering and the government powerless to protect the royal dead, and had been hidden all together, as a matter of precaution, in a secret shaft, where they lay until discovered by modern grave robbers, who in placing royal trinkets on the modern market betrayed themselves and inspired the search that resulted in bringing to light, in 1881, that marvelous array of mummies, including those of Seti I, Rameses the Great, and of the monarchs who had preceded and succeeded them upon the throne

HIS MAJESTY, AMENOPHIS II

of Thebes. Thus both the royal bodies and the royal tombs of the great dynasties were found, but the bodies were not found in these tombs, save in the case of one King — Amenophis II. One tomb was overlooked, both by the ancient ghouls and by the later Pharaoh who tried to save the bodies of his fathers by concealing them elsewhere. One tomb, therefore, remained untouched, until the men of science of our modern day, in 1898, found its hidden entrance, groped their way along its superbly decorated corridors, and, reaching the inmost mortuary chamber, looked on the face of one great King who had been lying there for three thousand three hundred and thirty-four years. Here he was found just as his courtiers had left him on the day of his imposing funeral in the year 1436 B. C. This was to me the most impressive moment that came to me in Egypt, this moment when I stood, almost alone, in this royal presence, deep in the caverned mass of those Egyptian cliffs, face to face with one who

THE PYLON OF EDFU

EDFU UNEARTHED

THE GREAT ROCK TEMPLE OF RAMESES II AT ABU SIMBEL IN NUBIA

EGYPT

had been King in Thebes more than a hundred years before Rameses the Great was born — one who had come directly from his golden throne in that now ruined city to this granite bed, beside which we, creatures of a day, stand dumb and silent, chilled by the sense of all the centuries that lie between this man and us.

But it is with a deep sense of relief that we find ourselves again out in the free air of to-day, continuing our voyage southward from Thebes, toward other mighty monuments that wait for us along the River Nile. Greatest, at least in the material majesty of its perfect preservation, is the enormous temple that rises at a place called Edfu. It dates from the times of the Ptolemies, the Greek successors of the Pharaohs, who ruled Egypt from Alexandria, where their throne was established by virtue of Alexander's conquest of the land. The pylon of Edfu is practically perfect. It lacks only the cornice to complete the skyline, and the four masts

ROYALTIES AND DEITIES AT KOM OMBO

or flag-poles that were once fixed in those four grooves in the façade. The figures cut deep in the same huge wall represent a big King smiting his little enemies, while little gods and goddesses look on approvingly. The Ptolemies were not free from the old self-advertising passion of the Pharaohs; they also used the spare walls of their temples to let the whole world know the deeds and titles by right of which they held the center of the stage.

The preservation of Edfu is due to the fact that it lay partly buried throughout the Middle Ages. An Arab village grew up in it and on top of it. Much labor and money has been spent in shoveling off and out the accumulations of two thousand years, until to-day Edfu stands disinterred. But the Arab town surrounds it, and, given a decade of neglect, would creep back and overwhelm the ruin with its rubbish heap of vileness. Happier the fate of the ruins that

KOM OMBO

AT ASSUAN

were buried in the clean sand of the desert. The beautiful ruin of Kom Ombo, forty miles farther south and on the east bank of the Nile, was covered until recently with the pure, sandy cloak thrown over it by the east winds from Arabia. To-day the columns have emerged like lovely flowers in stone from their age-long concealment. The coloring of the deep-cut reliefs is in some places startlingly bright and fresh. The graceful lines and exquisite proportions of the hall of columns tell of the influence of Greek art; all this was a creation of the Greek age in Egypt. The Greeks brought to the heavy and impressive architecture of old Egypt some of the lightness and grace that characterized the immortal creations of Greek art on Grecian soil. We know that brilliant color was freely used within these temples. Traces enough remain upon some of the gorgeous capitals to give us some idea of what the decoration of this temple must have been.

From Kom Ombo to the first cataract the distance is under thirty miles — and at the next stop there won't be any temple. We are at Assuan, the health resort *par excellence* of Egypt. It is the sanatorium of Africa. It is a glorious place for invalids, and the favorite resort for beggars from all parts of upper Egypt and the neighboring sandy wastes of Nubia. It is the headquarters of the "Backsheesh League"—a large delegation of which meets every steamer that ties up to the pierless banks of the Nile at Assuan. One secure refuge for the helpless tourist is the terrace of the Cataract Hotel, whence we enjoy a splendid view of the Nile cañon. The outside world beyond the brilliant Saracenic awnings that are stretched to attenuate the tropic glare is almost too gloriously bright and sunny. On one side lies the parched bed of the shrunken Nile, and on the other the sun-baked desert of Nubia begins. One of our first short excursions into this glaring region was to the ancient quarries whence the old Egyptians took the granite for their colossal statues and their everlasting obelisks. We find one obelisk still unseparated from the mother rock; shaped and finished on two sides, it has not yet been cut loose from the cliff. Marks on the rocks tell us how this was to have been done. Wedges of wood were driven into the holes bored all along the proposed line of separation; these wedges were

THE TERRACE OF THE CATARACT HOTEL

then wetted, the wood expanded, a great seam opened, and the block of granite was ready for shipment down the Nile to Thebes, Memphis, or Heliopolis. Not far from this birthplace of all the obelisks we find a settlement of Soudanese—the blackest black folk in all Africa. There, and in the adjacent settlement of Bisharins,

THE NILE AT ASSUAN

every one, from the boldest "warriors" down to the tiniest babies, is in the retail *backsheesh* business.

About four miles above Assuan the Nile is dammed by the new Barrage, a modern work that takes rank in magnitude with the great ancient monuments of Egypt. But where they were erected at the call of selfish pride, at the cost of many lives, and to the impoverishment of the nation, this work is the result of an endeavor on the part of a wise government to give life to hitherto dead areas, and to bring the possibility of wealth within the reach of the hitherto impoverished population. The dam is one mile and a

EGYPT

AN UNBORN OBELISK AT ASSUAN

quarter long from shore to shore. It controls, to a certain extent, the level of the lower Nile by holding in reserve the surplus waters of the annual inundation, diverting them into new irrigation canals or letting them escape in regulated flow through the sluices to the greatest advantage of every farm and field between here and the delta, six hundred miles below. It lightens the labor of the countless workers at the *shadufs*, who do not have to dip as deep as formerly. It also makes possible the irrigation of broad areas which until now were waterless and unproductive. It has of course suppressed the old First Cataract of the Nile, where formerly boats had to be hauled by hundreds of natives up through the raging rapids, an exciting, all-day undertaking. Now we steam

SOUDANESE DEFIANCE

quietly into a superb canal and are quickly lifted through four locks to the new level of the upper Nile.

The Nubian Nile above the cataract has been transformed into a rock-bound lake. The Great Barrage has backed the waters up, widening the river, engulfing the sites of villages, submerging islands and apparently transforming the tall palm trees into some

A "BATTLE" FOR THE TOURIST'S GOLD

new kind of water-plant. The "*Nemo*" one day capped the climax of her many absurd performances by getting stranded in the tree-tops of a grove of palms. There we ran out of coal, and there we lay for twenty-two hours, while a small boat went back to Shellal for a supply of fuel. But it was a delay that was delightful. Few yachtsmen can boast of a similar experience. Like Peter Pan, we dwell among the tree-tops; beneath us doubtless are the submerged ruins of some Nubian village, which once rose on some lost island of the Nubian Nile.

There was one world-famous island in this vanished archipelago — an island dear to every lover of the beautiful — the Isle of Philæ, crowned with temples and girdled with temple walls and colonnades. Isis was the deity adored at Philæ, and it is fitting that a goddess, not a god, should have been supreme here on this isle that was so sweetly feminine and so exquisitely beautiful. Of the island itself only one rocky eminence remains above the new Nile level. Of the temples much still remains in view. Philæ has become a beautiful Egyptian Venice — and comparing the floating Philæ of to-day with the regretted island Philæ of the past, it seems to me that lovely Philæ has gained in beauty through this inundation due to the building of the Great Barrage. Those who agree with me in preferring this new Venetian Philæ will

THE ASSUAN BARRAGE

bless the dam; those who do not, will — shall we say — "Barrage the dam!" At any rate the Nile now paves the courts and fills the sanctuaries with the freshness and the music of the living waters. If Philæ on dry land was dreamlike, Philæ afloat seems an enchantment, unfolding its manifold perfections as we glide

AMONG THE TREE-TOPS

silently and smoothly round about her pylons and her pillars, keeping always in view that most exquisite of all her structures, the columned *kiosk* known as Pharaoh's Bed. As we circle it by night, Philæ appears like an architectural wonderland moored in the moonlight on the bosom of the ancient stream. Yet there is sadness in the thought that what we see will not be seen by the travelers of future years. Philæ is doomed; the waters that lend her now this strange Venetian charm — the waters that have washed away the dirt and débris from her gates — will ultimately undermine her sacred walls

IN THE LOCKS

and wash away all save her sacred memory.

For nearly a hundred miles above the dam, the Nile appears to be in a perpetual state of flood. The shoreline has been pushed back, and all the trees in sight appear to have gone in wading, some of them waist-deep in the Nile waters. We are in Nubia, the Biblical land of Kush, where to this day the dwellers live in primitive simplicity. Small boys wear silver charms in place of shirts and little girls eke out their charms with fringy skirts called "Mother Nubias" that are too cute for anything. There is matter for a dozen lectures here in Nubia, where manners, customs, and beliefs are all so curious and strange.

PHARAOH'S BED AT PHILÆ

We note with interest the immemorial but to us novel way in which the women dress their hair; it looks for all the world like

ABOVE THE BARRAGE

THE TEMPLE OF ISIS

black or reddish fringe — for sometimes the braided tresses, stiffened with black Nile mud, are dyed a somber red. Near every town we find a temple in the neighboring desert, and near every temple some red-haired woman with a mud-framed face, who is sure to have a silver ring for sale. There are some fourteen temples between the first and second cataracts — one very like another — all impressive

FLOODED PHILÆ

PHILÆ, AN EGYPTIAN VENICE

because of their solitary situations, because of the desolation of the sandy wilderness out of which they lift their shattered forms like wrecks of prehistoric ships lost in the bed of a dead and dried-up ocean. We dutifully "did" all these temples. All are worth visiting, but the story of these visits would delay beyond reason our arrival at the place where we shall see the most impressive sight of the upper

THE KIOSK THAT WAS NEVER FINISHED

EGYPT

IN THE LAND OF KUSH

Nile, a sight that ranks with the Pyramids and the Sphinx as one among the three supreme wonders of this wonderland of Africa. The place is known to-day by the Arab name of Abu Simbel, which means "Father of the Ear of Corn." We speak of the wonderful works at Abu Simbel as "temples," but they should not be called temples; the word suggests to the traveler who has come thus far up the Nile, something ordinary, something commonplace. He has

ONE OF MANY NUBIAN TEMPLES

seen so many temples that one temple more or less means very little to him. He would perhaps gladly pass without a glance the wonders of this cliff-bound Nubian shore if they were nothing more than temples. Abu Simbel is a place of unique marvels, masterly creations of a genius whose originality and

IN NUBIA

daring were amazing, whose resources must have been practically limitless.

That genius was none other than Rameses the Great — great even here in savage Nubia three hundred miles above his capital and only forty miles from the Second Cataract of

A "MOTHER NUBIA"

EGYPT

the Nile, beyond which lay the country of the barbarians against whom he ofttimes sent his conquering hosts. Here at Abu Simbel the great King set his everlasting seal deep in the rocky face of Nubia, marking this desert province as his own forever. More than three thousand years have rolled along the valley of the Nile without effacing this deep-set seal of that indomitable monarch; and even were the cliffs at last worn smooth by the rough rubbing of the hand of Time, there would remain the vast interior halls of Abu Simbel hollowed in the living rock of these grim cliffs that loom above the ever-living Nile and at the same time form a rocky dam to hold in check the billows of the dead sandy sea of the Sahara that rolls in all its vastness

THE "NEMO" ON THE NUBIAN NILE

westward from their tops to the far-off dunes along the Moorish shores that front the wide Atlantic. We cannot see that desert from the river, but we know that it is there and we do see the broad cascade of sand that tumbles imperceptibly over the brink and slowly swells and spreads until it sometimes half conceals the sculptured façade of the greater cliff-shrine on the left. The lesser rock-cut sanctuary on the right is not so threatened by the overflow from that great sea of sand. Its six colossal figures stand forth, at all times clean and sharp, from the six niches where they have stood like stony sentries for over thirty-one long centuries. The four male figures represent great Rameses, the two female figures, Rameses' queen and wife, Nefretere, who was the only royal consort of old Egypt ever honored with colossal portraits rivaling in magnitude those of the male Pharaoh, her royal lord and master. This in fact might be called a family memorial glorifying the wife of Rameses and the offspring of Rameses, for lost in the shadows beside the huge thirty-three-foot

ABU SIMBEL

likenesses of the royal pair, stand comparatively tiny figures representing their royal daughters, the princesses Meryt-Ammon and Hent-tewe, and their royal sons, the princes Mery-Atum, Mery-Re Amen-her-khopshef, and Ra-her-wnamf! What a time the royal herald must have had announcing the members of this royal

THE RAMESES FAMILY

family as they appeared upon the scene at the great ceremonies of the Theban court! The door admits us to the cave-like rooms cut in the cliff — a hypostyle hall, a transverse chamber, and an inner closet-sanctuary where stands a striking relief of the goddess Hathor in the form of a sacred cow. Human heads of Hathor and incised pictures and hieroglyphs adorn the pillars and the walls of these dark man-made caverns from whose cool depths we look out upon the hot sun-kissed surface of the silent Nile.

This lesser wonder would be alone well worth the journey. What shall we say of the greater wonder — the great rock-cut

IN THE HATHOR SHRINE

shrine before which sit the four colossi, as they have sat throughout the thirty-one hundred years that have elapsed since they were born, gazing benignly eastward, greeting the sun whose god was worshiped in that sanctuary, the doors of which they will guard until the earth itself shall pass away? There they must sit, doomed to terrestrial immortality by the pride and egotism of the King who fashioned them in his own image — for the four giants are four portraits of Rameses the Great.

THE NILE AT ABU SIMBEL

EGYPT

They are each sixty-five feet high. Should they arise they would almost overtop the cliff of which they are a part. Each holds a little desert in his lap, the feet of each are bathed in the hot desert sands that come down from the dammed and pent Sahara just above. The glacier-like sand-drift which at one time almost concealed the whole of Abu Simbel is fed by

RAMESES IN COLOSSAL QUADRUPLICATE

the exhaustless sandy reservoir of the Sahara. Fast as it is removed, faster it comes, but silently and imperceptibly, dancing down from the high desert with every breath of hot wind from the west. This we discovered as we toiled toward the top to peer over the cliff summits and see where all the sand was coming from. Viewed from a higher level on this sandy slope, the faces of the giants show their profiles grandly in relief against the golden cliff. The nearer statue of the southernmost pair has lost its head, decapitated by an earthquake soon after it was carved. The other giants still retain their heads, their crowns, and that expression of thoughtful unconcern that usually distinguishes the

THE KINGLY PROFILES

portraits of the Pharaohs. Eight other colossal images of Rameses adorn the cavernous interior. The inner walls are all adorned with pictures that illustrate, and hieroglyphs that glorify the deeds of Rameses; it would require days to read the stories that they tell. On the north wall is an enormous composition — a picture of the Battle of Kadesh, where Rameses, in his chariot, cut off from his own forces, yet by his kingly prowess routed the entire army of his enemies, the Hittites. But all this is very difficult to make out because of the darkness that prevails, for there are no windows — only one great door. We stand at the threshold and peer into the dimly lighted series of halls and corridors. It is a hundred and eighty feet from the threshold to the figures of four gods who sit in the far inner

THE PHARAONIC FALSE BEARD AND
DOUBLE CROWN

EGYPT

NILE GODS UNITING THE PAPYRUS AND THE LILY

shrine; the gods themselves as well as their simple throne being a part of the solid rock. All this is not architecture, it is artistic tunneling. The huge figures of Osiris that support the roof are integral portions of the mountain inside of which we stand; the ceiling, walls, and

THE PORTAL OF THE GREAT ROCK-SHRINE

portals are of living rock. The eight colossi are in the form of eight likenesses of Rameses, the farthest one on the right being the finest portrait of the King extant. It is undoubtedly a portrait; we can trace resemblance to the actual face of Rameses as we saw it lying in mummy case in Cairo.

To that figure I owe one of those great moments that come so rarely to the traveler, one of those thrills that are the chief rewards of travel, one of those instants longest remembered and most frequently recalled. It came at sunrise one morning late in February. We stood in the great portal gazing into the dim sanctuary. Behind us the Nile, beyond which rose the eastern hills outlined against the glow of the coming day. The sun leaps in sudden glory above the crests, and sends its first ray straight as an arrow

THE VAST INTERIOR HALLS OF ABU SIMBEL

EGYPT

into the holy place that Rameses hollowed in this Nubian cliff. That first flash of the new-born day pierces the darkness of this caverned sanctuary and smites the four gods there in the inmost shrine full in their stony faces. It was a vivid, thrilling

THE FIRST FLASH OF DAY

thing, to see the bright glory of the newest to-day touch and make luminous the dark mystery of this shrine of oldest yesterday. Then, slowly, and yet so quickly that we can *see* it move, that rectangular patch of glory, glowing white, moves from left to right as the rising sun begins its journey toward the southern skies. And as it moves the shadows gather on the left again, and other shadows, those that shroud that perfect likeness of King Rameses — those peopled shadows on the right — retire, slowly and yet so quickly that at a given instant Great Rameses seems to start forward out from the black depths of the centuries, and for a few uncanny seconds seems to live and breathe again, trans-

RAMESES THE GREAT TRANSFIGURED
BY THE SUN

figured by the glory of the God of the Day — the great God of the Sun, all holy Ammon Ra, to whom the Pharaoh had dedicated this and a hundred other temples thousands of years ago. This instant marked the climax of our journey, but not our jour-

WADY HALFA

A TINTED TOMMY ATKINS

ney's end. Southward for forty miles we cruise to Wady Halfa, once an important port through which the commerce of the Soudan had to pass. Now, owing to the completion of the Soudan railway to the shore of the Red Sea, and the opening of the maritime port of Suakin, this river port of Wady Halfa loses much of its importance. It remains, however, the northern terminus of the railway to Khartum, about five hundred miles away, and it will figure on the time-card of the Cape to Cairo line when all the missing links of that chain of railways shall have been forged and joined together — but that's another story.

Our travel tale of Egypt ends a few miles south of Wady Halfa, at the Second Cataract of the great river to which Egypt owes her very being. From the bold pinnacle of the Rock

OUR JOURNEY'S END

of Abusir we look down upon the so-called cataract which is not a cataract, as we understand the word. It is simply a series of rapids where the Nile fights its way through a wild outcropping of blackish rock. Gazing southward, we see the beginning of that region of mystery and tragedy — the terrible Soudan — the conquest of which was begun by the

THE SECOND "CATARACT"

Pharaohs, attempted by the Romans, and finally achieved by the English under Kitchener. That the old Egyptian rulers even dreamed of conquest there proves them to have been men as ambitious as the most ambitious of our modern empire builders. Their works which we have seen in Egypt and in Nubia prove that they were masters of arts, and commanded resources of which we of to-day are ignorant. Great Kings they were, great works they have bequeathed to Egypt and to us, for we, the free man of a free land of to-day, are the heirs of all that was worth while in that king-ridden, priest-ridden, slave-ridden Egypt of a great dark yesterday. In Egypt and in modern Europe men look toward the past, and therefore ancient monuments may have for them greater significance than they can ever have for us, for we are looking always toward the future. We may roam afar and mingle with the children of the past in the old lands of the older hemisphere, interested or amazed by the things that they find great, but when it comes to living our real lives and doing our real work we turn with eagerness toward the new hemisphere, content to live and work among our fellow-countrymen, who are the heirs of a great yesterday, the masters of a wonderful to-day, and the makers of a still more wonderful to-morrow.

RAMESES, HIS MARK

FURTHER READING

John Anthony West's *The Traveller's Key to Ancient Egypt: A Guide to the Sacred Places of Ancient Egypt* (1995) makes an interesting comparison to Holmes's 1906 travelogue. Eugene Fodor's *Egypt* (1996) also provides interesting historical information. For an overall view of the Middle East at the turn of the century, see the appropriate chapters in Bernard Lewis's *The Middle East* (1995).

The history of Egypt and that of Europe 100 years ago are intertwined. Anyone who wishes to find out about the major events and personalities of Europe between 1875 and 1914 should read Eric Hobsbawn's *The Age of Empire: 1875-1914* (1989). Other interesting books on the period include *Europe 1815-1914* by Gordon Craig; James Joll's *Europe Since 1870;* and *A Survey of European Civilization* (Vol. II, from 1660), by Wallace K. Ferguson and Geoffrey Brown. See also: Barbara Tuchman, *The Proud Tower* (1966); Edward R. Tannenbaum, *1900: The Generation Before the Great War* (1976); and *War by Timetable: How the First World War Began* (1969), *The Struggle for Mastery in Europe, 1848-1918* (1971), and *The Last of Old Europe: A Grand Tour* (1976), by A. J. P. Taylor.

—Dr. Fred L. Israel

CONTRIBUTORS

General Editor FRED L. ISRAEL is an award-winning historian. He received the Scribe's Award from the American Bar Association for his work on the Chelsea House series *The Justices of the United States Supreme Court*. A specialist in American history, he was general editor for Chelsea's *1897 Sears Roebuck Catalog*. Dr. Israel has also worked in association with Arthur M. Schlesinger, jr. on many projects, including *The History of U.S. Presidential Elections* and *The History of U.S. Political Parties*. He is senior consulting editor on the Chelsea House series *Looking into the Past: People, Places, and Customs,* which examines past traditions, customs, and cultures of various nations.

Senior Consulting Editor ARTHUR M. SCHLESINGER, JR. is the preeminent American historian of our time. He won the Pulitzer Prize for his book *The Age of Jackson* (1945), and again for *A Thousand Days* (1965). This chronicle of the Kennedy Administration also won a National Book Award. He has written many other books, including a multi-volume series, *The Age of Roosevelt*. Professor Schlesinger is the Albert Schweitzer Professor of Humanities at the City University of New York, and has been involved in several other Chelsea House projects, including the *American Statesmen* series of biographies on the most prominent figures of early American history.

IRVING WALLACE (1916-1990), whose essay on Burton Holmes is reprinted in the forward to The World 100 Years Ago, is one of the most widely read authors in the world. His books have sold over 200 million copies, and his best-sellers include *The Chapman Report, The Prize, The Man, The Word, The Second Lady,* and *The Miracle*.

INDEX

Abbas II Hilmi, Khedive, 38
Abu Simbel, 155-66
Abusir, Rock of, 167
Abydos, Necropolis of, 112-18, 120
Agriculture, 100-102, 104-5
Aïda, 48
Alexander the Great, 42, 143
Alexandria
  architectural ruins in, 41-42
  English rule in, 39
  port of, 40-41
  route to Cairo, 44-45
Ali, Mohammed, 65-69
Amenophis III, 123-25
  statues of, at Thebes, 134-35
  tomb of, at Thebes, 140
Ammon Ra
  cult of, 121-22
  priests of, 80-81
  temple at Abu Simbel, 155-66
  temple at Karnak, 127-32
  worship at Abydos, 114
Amr, Mosque of, 58-59
Antiquities, 74
Area, inhabitable, 103-4
Assiut, 105-9
  cemetery of, 105-9
  dam near, 105
  depth of Nile above, 109-10
  housing in, 107
Assuan, 145-48

Bab en Nasr (gate), 63-64
Backsheesh, 102-103.
  See also Beggars
Bargaining, 50-51
Barkuk, 62
Beggars
  at Assiut, 106
  at Assuan, 145-47
  for English books, 108-9
  at ports, 102-3
Bisharins, 147
Blindness, 107-8
Boats
  Dahabiyeh, 94-95
  felucca, 98-99
  steamers, 95-96, 109-12
Botti, Dr., 42

Cairo
  Bab en Nasr, 63-64
  bazaars of, 51-52
  call to prayer in, 60-61
  modern buildings of, 82
  modernization of, 47-50
  National Museum, 73-79
  peddlers in, 49-51
  population of, 45
  route to Alexandria, 44-45
  wealthy tourists in, 47
Canals, 44
Cemeteries, visiting, 106-7
Cheops, pyramid of, 84-87
Children
  condition of, 107-8
  Nubian, 152
Christianity, 42. *See also* Copts
Copts, 96-97
Cromer, Lord Evelyn, 38-39
Crops, 104

Dahabiyeh. See under Boats
Dams
  above Assuan, 147-52
  near Assiut, 105
Demographics, 45, 103
Dendera, shrine at, 118-21

Edfu, 143-45
El Azhar, Mosque of, 52
Embalming, 77-79
Engineering, ancient, 84-85
England
  effect on enterprise, 104-5

obelisk in London, 81
  as plenipotentiary, 37-39
Evil Eye, the, 107-8
Excursion steamers. *See under* Boats
Eye diseases, 107-8

Farming, 100-102, 104-5
Fellahin. See Irrigation
Felucca. See under Boats
Forced labor, 110-11

Gates. *See* Bab en Nasr
Gods and goddesses
  Ammon, 121-22
  depicted in art, 115
  Harmachis, 114
  Hathor, 119
  Horus, 114
  Isis, 114, 150
  Ptah, 114
  relationship to kings, 115
Granite, 146
Grave robbers, 139-40
Greeks, influence of, 145
Guides, for pyramids, 87

Hall of the Kings, 116-18
Hathor, shrine of, 118-21
Hatshepsut, Queen, 135-36
Health resorts, 145
Heaven. *See* Paradise
Heliopolis, 80-82

Hieroglyphics
  and Coptic language, 96-97
  in Temple of Osiris at Abydos, 115-16
Holy Carpet. *See* Mahmal
Hotels
  Cataract, at Assuan, 146
  at Luxor, 122
  Shepheard's (Cairo), 46-47

Ibrahim Pasha, 48
Indigestion, cure for, 59
Irrigation, 100-102, 104-5, 148
Ismail Pasha, 48

Jewelry, of King Menes, 117
Judaism, 56

Karnak, 80, 120
Kings, Hall of the, 116-18
kiosks, 151
Kitchener, Horatio, 168
Kom Ombo (temple), 145
Koran, the, 48

Labor, forced, 110-11
Languages
  of the Copts, 97
  English, 108-9
Lighthouse (Alexandria), 43

Livestock, 106-7
Loti, Pierre, 90
Luxor, 122-23, 127. *See also* Thebes

Mahmal (Holy Carpet), 69-73
Mamelukes
  massacre by Mohammed Ali, 66-68
  mosques of, 62-63
Markets, 106-7
Mastaba. See Tombs
Mausoleums, of Mamaluke Sultans, 62-63
Mecca, 69-73
Medina, 69-73
Memphis, cemetery of, 91-93
Menes, King, 93, 116-17
Mohammed, 56
Mohammed Ali, 65-69
Money
  Backsheesh, 102-103
  payment for forced labor, 111
  reverence for, 50-51
Moslems
  beliefs of, 55-58
  meaning of term, 53
  visiting the dead, 106-7
Mosques
  attendance at, 59-60
  call to prayer in, 60-61

173

description of, 55
of El Amr, 58-59
of El Azhar, 52
of Mameluke Sultans, 61-63
of Mohammed Ali, 64-65
muezzin, 60-61
Mummies, 74
  at Abydos, 113
  hidden, 138-40
  at Memphis, 91-92
  of Rameses, 136
Museum, National, 73-79

Nile River, the
  Arabian shore of, 99
  Assuan dam on, 147-49
  Cataracts of, 148-49, 167
  and irrigation, 100-102
  islands in, 150-52
  Libyan shore of, 99
  navigating, 109-12, 149
  Nubian, 149, 152
  travel on, 94-102
  winds and currents, 99-100
Nubia, 146, 152

Obelisks
  at Assuan, 146-47
  at Heliopolis, 80-82
  in modern cities, 81
Officials, fear of, 110
Opera House (Cairo), 48
Osiris
  desire for burial near, 113
  figures at Abu Simbel, 163
  temple at Abydos, 113-15

Paradise, 56-57
Peddlers, 49-51
Petrified trees, 64
Pharaoh's Bed, 151
Pharos (lighthouse), 43
Philæ, Isle of, 149-52
Pilgrimages
  to cemetery at Assiut, 106-7
  to Mecca and Medina, 69-73
Plato, 80-81
Pompey's Pillar, 41-42
Poverty, 102
Profit motive, 104-5
Prophets, Moslem, 56
Ptolemies, the, 143-44
Pyramids, 82-88
  of Cheops, 84-87
  of Kephren, 87-88
  at Memphis, 92-93
  Step, at Sakkara, 93

Railroads
  Alexandria to Cairo, 44-45
  Cape to Cairo, 166-67
  Soudan to the Red Sea, 166
Rameses II. *See* Rameses the Great
Rameses the Great
  and Abu Simbel, 156-66
  family of, 158-59
  mummy of, 77-79, 136, 139-40
  statue at Memphis, 93-94
  statues of, at Thebes, 127
  and temple at Thebes, 125-27
  and Temple of Osiris at Abydos, 113-14
Religious beliefs
  of ancient Egyptians, 76-77
  of Moslems, 55-58
Romans
  Emperor Theodosius, 42
  and the Soudan, 168
Roumeleh Square (Cairo), 70

Sakiyeh. *See* Irrigation
School, American, 108
Seraphis, Temple of, 42
Servants, 92
Seti the First
  coffin of, 79
  listed in Hall of the

Kings, 116-17
mummy of, 78-79, 139
and Temple of Osiris at Abydos, 113-15
Shadufs. See Irrigation
Sheik of the Village, 74-77
Slavery, 83-88. *See also* Labor, forced
Soudan, the, 167-68
Soudanese, 147
Spencer, Herbert, 108
Sphinx, the, 88-90
Statues
   of Amenophis III, 134-35
   of Ibrahim Pasha, 48
   of Osiris, 163
   the Sheik of the Village, 74-77
   the Vocal Memnon, 135
Steamers. *See under* Boats
Suakin (port), 166
Suez Canal, opening of, 48

Superstitions
   burial at Abydos, 113
   Evil Eye, 107-8

Temples
   Abu Simbel, 155-66
   of Amenophis III, at Luxor, 123-25
   at Edfu, 143-45
   of Hathor at Dendera, 118-21
   of Hatshepsut, 136
   at Isle of Philæ, 150
   Kom Ombo, 145
   Nubian, 153-56
   of Osiris at Abydos, 113-15
   ruins at Karnak, 127-32
   of Seraphis, 42
Tewfik, Khedive, 38
Thebes, 122-27, 132-43
Theodosius, Emperor, 42
Thotmes III, 80
Tombs. *See also* Pyramids
   of Amenophis III, 134, 140-43
   at Memphis, 91-92
   underground, at Thebes, 136-38
Tourists, wealthy, 45-47

Universities
   of El Azhar (Cairo), 52-55
   of priests of Ammon, 80-81
Ushabti. See Servants

Vandalism
   of ancient ruins, 82, 88
   grave robbers, 139-40
Verdi, Guiseppe, 48
Victory, Gate of. *See* Bab en Nasr
Vocal Memnon, 135

Wady Halfa, 166
Water. *See* Irrigation
Waterfalls, 148-49, 167
Women
   hairstyles of Nubian, 152-53
   role of, 56-57, 59, 127

MACARIO GARCIA MIDDLE SCHOOL

3 3396 01200210 4   916.204 HOL

Egypt

DATE DUE			

916.204
HOL

3 3396 01200210 4
Holmes, Burton.

Egypt

MACARIO GARCIA MIDDLE SCHOOL

804923 02995   28123C   040